NO
EXIT

THE BIG EMPTY Series

The Big Empty

Paradise City

Desolation Angels

No Exit

THE BIG EMPTY

NO

EXIT

BY
J.B. STEPHENS

razOr
bill

The Big Empty 4: No Exit

RAZORBILL

Published by the Penguin Group
Penguin Young Readers Group
345 Hudson Street, New York, New York 10014, U.S.A.
Penguin Group (USA) Inc., 375 Hudson Street, New York, New York 10014, U.S.A.
Penguin Books Canada Ltd, 10 Alcorn Avenue, Toronto, Ontario, Canada M4V 3B2
(a division of Pearson Penguin Canada, Inc.)
Penguin Books Ltd, 80 Strand, London WC2R 0RL, England
Penguin Ireland, 25 St Stephen's Green, Dublin 2, Ireland
(a division of Penguin Books Ltd)
Penguin Group (Australia), 250 Camberwell Road, Camberwell,
Victoria 3124, Australia (a division of Pearson Australia Group Pty Ltd)
Penguin Books India Pvt Ltd, 11 Community Centre, Panchsheel Park,
New Delhi – 110 017, India
Penguin Group (NZ), Cnr Airborne and Rosedale Roads, Albany,
Auckland 1310, New Zealand (a division of Pearson New Zealand Ltd)
Penguin Books (South Africa) (Pty) Ltd, 24 Sturdee Avenue, Rosebank,
Johannesburg 2196, South Africa

Penguin Books Ltd, Registered Offices: 80 Strand, London WC2R 0RL, England

10 9 8 7 6 5 4 3 2 1

Interior design by Christopher Grassi

Library of Congress Cataloging-in-Publication Data is available

NO
EXIT

ONE

"MOM? IT'S KEELY."

There was nothing but silence on the other end, so long that Keely was afraid the connection had been cut, or her mom had hung up, or she hadn't even been heard.

Finally—a drawn breath. Even a thousand miles away she could hear the catch in it. "Keely? Are you all right?"

She didn't ask, "Is it really you?" or cry, or have hysterics, or say, "Oh my God, it really *is* you." Keely almost smiled—that was Mom: succinct, rational, and right to the point.

"I'm fine, Mom."

Now the mother questions. "Where were you? Where the *hell* have you been?"

"It's kind of a long story, but I'm okay. . . ." The others showed up quietly next to her: Michael, Irene, Diego, and Liza. She had walked away from them before, taken off to the call center with the vouchers and no explanations. Michael nodded, understanding immediately what she was doing and why. She could always rely on him for that.

"I was worried sick about you, Keely! You disappeared and I thought you were dead! It's been months! The police couldn't find you. . . ."

"You were *worried* about me?" Keely growled, remembering why she had left in the first place. "That's a new one. Before I left, you hardly knew that I existed."

"Don't be so childish," her mom snapped, but there were tears in her voice. "You don't know the pressure I was under, the work I had to do. . . ."

"Yeah, we should talk about exactly what kind of work you *do* sometime," Keely muttered. The annoying little Slattery suck-up Jane had implied that Dr. Gilmore was not just working in triage as she had claimed, but was employed by the government for more nefarious purposes. "I left you notes, I tried to talk to you—I even made you frigging *dinner* every night!"

Irene gave her a worried look—Diego and Liza stepped back. Keely knew they'd never witnessed her so angry, were probably surprised to hear her talking to her mom this way.

Again there was silence on the other end; it didn't frighten Keely as much this time.

"You're right," her mother finally said. "I've been thinking about that a lot the last few months. How I couldn't stop the loss of my husband and one of my daughters, but I could have prevented losing you."

"Well, you haven't lost me yet," Keely conceded, surprised by her mother's admission. "Though you almost *did*, several times, permanently."

"Don't say that."

"It's true, though. I was—"

Michael reached over and put his hand over the receiver before she could continue, shaking his head at her.

"What?" Keely hissed. She couldn't believe he was interrupting her first real conversation with her mom in almost a year. This was more than they had said to each other about real things practically since her sister had died. "My mom's not going to 'tell' on us!"

"The line might be tapped," Michael whispered.

Oh. That made sense. Chastised, Keely pulled the phone back away from him. "Sorry, Mom. I can't tell you right now."

"Where are you?"

"Houston."

Michael rolled his eyes and shook his head.

"Where? I'll come get you."

"I . . . don't want to come home right now, Mom. But there are things I want to talk to you about." Suddenly she realized exactly what her mom had said. "What do you mean, you'll come get me? It'll take days for you to get here, even if you have a car and all the permits. And the buses are even slower."

Her mom sighed deeply. "There's a lot both of us need to talk about. Let's just say I know the right people and can *fly* there."

Flying? *Now?* Impossible. No one flew anymore except for the ultra-rich, and the government, and very important people. . . .

"What did she say?" Michael demanded, seeing the look on Keely's face.

"Tell me where I can meet you," her mom prodded again.

"I don't know . . . uh . . ." Keely thought hard, running through everything she had ever heard about Houston. It wasn't a lot. "Remember where Bree wanted to go? When you went to that conference? I'll check there, every day starting tomorrow, at dusk. Go alone."

"Bree . . . ?"

But before her mom could make any other protests, or disagree, or question further, Keely ended the call. "I love you," she whispered softly, and hung up the phone.

"What was all that about?" Michael asked.

"The Children's Museum," Keely said a little sadly, remembering her sister's excitement about getting to go there—more than to the space center. She sucked in her breath, trying not to tear up.

"It had a really cool gift shop," Irene said, sympathizing and changing the subject at the same time. "I used to go whenever we visited Aunt Marie."

"I hope this was the right thing to do," Liza murmured, studying Keely. "And I can't believe you called her and gave up our location without even running the plan by any of us."

Michael nodded. "What did I say?"

"But I trust her," Keely said firmly. "And she thinks she can fly here. She knows some people in power."

"Exactly," Diego said, his eyes dark with disapproval. "And we've all seen how power destroys things."

"Let's just wait this out," Keely said. "Give her a chance." As they filed out of the call center to the plaza that had once held shops and restaurants, Keely hoped she was right. She could trust her mother . . . couldn't she?

TWO

DR. CATHERINE GILMORE HUNG UP THE PHONE AND STARED AT it quietly. No expression showed on her pale, freckled face, but her mind was whirling, cogs and gears trying out all the possibilities of what to do next before spitting out the right answer, before she acted.

Her private office was luxurious by hospital standards, filled with all sorts of expensive heavy hardwood and brushed-steel furniture. A few cool halogen and LED lights distributed artfully around the room made it seem almost like a library or academic office, good for thinking, good for reading, good for talking to students and discussing philosophy. If she'd cared, she would have piled up some books somewhere.

A peace offering, a bribe from the people who basically held her hostage.

Not that she would have left, even if she could have. That was the horrible thing about it.

Outside, dusk was settling as silently as the rest of the day had come and gone. Although she had never worked there before Strain 7, Gilmore was pretty sure that it would have been a lot different then: a redder sky from more pollution, either traffic racing by or stuck still beneath the palm trees that lined the streets, the occasional musical honks from gang-modded cars, poor people waiting for the bus at a bench. That had always infuriated her—the obvious rift between the haves and have-nots, the stream of PT Cruisers and Ferraris and Ford GTs and Cabrios and even Rolls-Royces headed back to their cozy homes in the hills, while their housekeepers began the slow journey home by woefully unsupported public transportation.

Now she would have given almost anything to see that stream of bright-colored, angry cars, rather than the few that crept by fearfully. And no one waited for the bus.

"Dr. Gilmore?" A young man stuck his head in. He had a sheaf of papers in his hands. "I have the results from group 7b-5. . . ."

"I have to go away for a few days, Sanjay." Dr. Gilmore decided as she said it, staring at the phone on her desk. "I just heard from my daughter."

"Oh my God—is she okay?"

"I think so. But I want to go get her." Information—

but no extra details. Everyone was working for a common cause here, and no one particularly liked the employers, but you could never be sure who had a big mouth or who had something to gain by spilling a little. Sanjay, bless his heart, would tell everyone about Keely, out of excitement and genuine happiness for his boss. Those who were filled with less . . . *goodwill* would then be on equal information terms with everyone else. How can you sell a secret when it isn't a secret? "I'm going to request emergency travel papers and flight coupons."

"My sister works on the base," Sanjay offered. "She can tell you which troop carriers are headed wherever you need to go."

"Thanks. But I'm hoping that the boys and girls upstairs feel that they owe me."

He nodded. "Don't worry—I'll work these results through and make up a report for you by the time you get back. I think we also can get started on the other group—if, uh, we manage to get the monkeys from the zoo."

Dr. Gilmore suddenly remembered a sunny day with her two daughters and husband at the—well, pretty awful—L.A. zoo. Keely had been up in arms about how the monkeys were held in captivity (she was a vegetarian that month) and then suddenly one of them dropped down right in front of her and cocked its head—like it was trying to figure out what her problem was. Bree had screamed with laughter, and even Keely had smiled, laughing at herself.

Those had actually been tamarinds. These were rhesus. She wondered if Keely would still object. . . .

"Thanks, Sanjay. You're the best."

After he left, she turned back to the phone, took a deep breath, and made the call.

THREE

". . . YES. I HAD THOUGHT SHE RAN AWAY OR WAS DEAD. SHE just called me—from Texas. I was wondering if I could requisition a flight and papers to go pick her up."

"That won't be easy," said the man taking the call.

The two people listening in on the speaker phone exchanged a nod.

"I'll tell them to give it to her," the woman whispered. The man nodded back. Then she pulled out her own phone, sleek and black and connected via satellite. "This is Abercrombie. Get me Tony—we're letting Catherine Gilmore go walkabout for her daughter and need follow-up in Houston. Who do we have there . . . ?"

FOUR

"MICHAEL SEEMS A LITTLE . . . DIFFERENT THESE DAYS, DOESN'T he?" Irene said, halfway done with the pile of corn on the table that needed husking. They'd been told it was "cattle corn," a little smaller and stockier than the corn her dad sometimes made on the grill for them in summer, but with her stomach growling, it didn't matter much.

She, Liza, and Diego were working on making dinner while Keely and Michael were out, gathering info and surveiling the place where they would meet Dr. Gilmore. It was a quiet, almost homey afternoon, with the little TV she'd found in her aunt's closet flickering quietly, showing reruns and government shows in black and white with the sound turned down.

It was just as well that Keely and Michael were away until dinner; her aunt's apartment wasn't really big enough for all five of them there at once. Quarters were definitely cramped; Irene and Diego were sharing a room and Michael had taken the couch—which meant that Keely and Liza had to share. Which Irene felt kind of bad about, but she wasn't going to offer to switch. Though the first morning Keely had come out *awfully* grumpy . . .

"Yeah, he sure seems to be back in his own in the big city," Diego said with a drawl. As she should have guessed, there was no end of talent in the boy who lived by himself for so long. He was chopping vegetables like a pro and arguing with Liza about what herbs would be good in what was basically an over-glorified winter vegetable succotash.

Of course, Irene was still not entirely clear on the concept of what exactly a succotash was.

Diego leaned against the counter with no help from his crutch—she'd tried to help both him and Michael. Michael had gotten frostbite on his foot when he was caught out in the wild, and Diego's lameness had been brought about by a soldier from "civilization"—but in the end Irene was just glad he was healing. They had managed to find a real doctor that afternoon and traded some of Diego's remaining bullets for a black-market examination. *Doctors without borders*, Irene thought ironically. The old man had winced when he saw Diego's wound and how badly it had healed—then *cut the whole thing open again*, cut out some of the damaged tissue, packed it full of ointment, bandaged it, and actually given them a bottle of real antibiotics. "Can't give you painkillers," he had apologized. "The soldiers get them first."

Already it looked like it had made a difference, though—and there was a bottle of extra-strength Tylenol in Irene's aunt's nightstand.

"Yeah. Five minutes in town and he's already making friends and charting our next course," Liza mused. She didn't sound *quite* as worshipful as she had just a few weeks ago. Irene was glad that the girl seemed to have gotten over her misgivings about leaving Novo Mundum, even with the journey as awful as it was. On the other hand, Irene also kind of wished that Liza had joined Michael and Keely on their outing—Irene and Diego hadn't had any real time alone since that first time they'd kissed. And watching him stand there, and crack jokes, and toss his boyish mop of hair out of his face . . .

"You know, Diego, now that we're in civilization, we should get you a proper haircut," Liza said, indicating his bangs with her knife.

Diego ducked behind Irene. "Over my dead body," he teased.

Wait, was she flirting *with Diego again?*

Irene continued shucking, not quite sure how to take Liza. None of them were. Although the former princess of Novo Mundum had pulled her weight throughout their escape, some of the vestiges of royalty remained. Irene was never one to tiptoe around, but considering everything Liza had left behind and Michael's meltdown, she wanted to give the girl some space. Besides, Diego was just playing with her, wielding an ear of corn like a sword, when something on the TV caught Irene's eye. "Look at that," she said, leaning over to turn it up.

". . . thousands of dissidents in Atlanta stormed the government buildings at Capitol Square this morning . . ." The images were so pre–Strain 7, so before anything Irene could remember in her lifetime, it was weird to watch, like a news story about another country or on a science-fiction show. Thousands of protesters *really were* marching down the streets, angry and screaming—though it was obvious that the government cameraman had chosen to focus on the crazier ones. Their T-shirts and signs were blurred out, pixilated beyond recognition, but when the camera turned quickly, one unmistakably said something like OUT WITH MACCAULEY.

"Holy crow," Diego said, whistling.

"They're letting them do this?" Liza murmured.

"Um, apparently not." Irene sighed as the camera swung back and showed ranks of helmeted and shielded military, MacCauley's guards, who fell somewhere between policemen and soldiers, bearing down on the protesters. Some troops just used their mass and weight; others had tear gas and heavy-pressure water hoses. The camera cut quickly to a worried-looking Government Broadcasting Network spokescaster.

". . . believe these agitators are acting largely in response to the government's decision to continue to delay local and national elections until the situation is more under control . . . In other news, an eighty-year-old woman's missing dog, lost since before Strain 7, made a miraculous return to her this morning. We turn to GBN's local affiliate station for the rest of the story. . . ."

"'Delay.'" Diego snorted. "How about 'cancel'?"

"People are actually *doing* something," Irene murmured, the tiniest ray of hope flickering in the darker corners of her head.

"I've never seen so many people in one spot in my life," Diego said, turning back to finish cooking supper. "Scary!"

"What's the point?" Liza asked, sounding a little like the old Liza. "The government's just going to stop them—and hurt a lot of people along the way."

"The point is that America is a *democracy*—or was—and people are finally speaking out. We didn't really elect MacCauley the first time, and we certainly don't want him in for a *second* term. Look what he's done to us!"

"But we've been in a state of emergency," Liza said slowly, though it was obvious she was actually listening to what Irene said. "Doesn't that change everything? Don't governments and things have to act different in times like this?"

"No, it doesn't, and no, they don't. Not this extremely," Irene said a little heatedly. Liza was such a child sometimes. "You don't change your whole constitution and government when an emergency pops up.

That's not what democracy is about—or living in a 'free country.'"

"You tell her, Citizen Margolis," Diego said appreciatively.

Irene smiled up at him and he smiled back, that warm, lazy grin that showed part of his crooked tooth.

"Whatever," Liza said, rolling a shucked ear of corn onto the counter. "That's done. I'm going outside for some air."

Irene wasn't sure whether the girl felt uncomfortable with her civics lecture or about the look that had passed between Diego and her, but she was glad to hear the door slam, relieved to feel Diego's arm slip around her waist and pull her close to his warm, tall body.

Thank you, Irene thought, thinking that Liza might be more perceptive than they gave her credit for.

FIVE

THE LINE SNAKED OUT INTO THE WAITING ROOM AND AROUND and around itself, the weather outside too cold and frozen even for the usually stoic Novo Mundians. Jonah noticed quite a few attractive girls his age that he hadn't before, confined as he was to the basements and plumbing fixtures and electrical boxes . . . and thought about Irene.

Of course, he missed her and hoped she was okay— even prayed, though it wasn't exactly Novo Mundum practice or policy. Jonah refused to believe that she and the others had been killed by the Slash. Okay, maybe Michael and his big mouth, but Irene was an up-and-coming *doctor*. Surely even barbarians like the Slash could see the use in keeping her alive. He bet they'd even figured out a way to escape.

That was his belief, and he was sticking to it until reality proved without a doubt that he was either right or wrong.

In the meantime, he found himself looking around for new friends. Everyone was bundled up or unbundling for the doctor's visit, unrolling yards-long homemade scarves and pulling homemade sweaters over their heads, sometimes accidentally lifting their shirts with them. . . .

"Jonah!"

Dr. MacTavish's voice cut clearly and harshly through the room. People smiled and stepped aside for him. Besides the usual politeness, he had earned a little something extra for figuring out how to get a bit more hot water in the winter with homebuilt solar collectors. It cut across all age, race, and gender preference lines: *everyone* likes hot showers. Jonah walked proudly forward, trying not to think about what was going to happen next.

Behind the desk Dr. MacTavish was preparing a needle, and Nurse Chong was checking something off on a long list, printed out on old-fashioned connected tractor-feed paper. *Wonder where they found boxes of that . . .* Nothing was wasted at Novo Mundum, and everything was recycled. There were a lot of jokes about that, especially when toilet paper ran low in between scouting missions.

"Hey, our hot-water hero!" the doctor said, smiling through tired eyes.

"Yes, ma'am," Jonah said, extending his arm.

"Just a minute—we're not quite ready yet." Dr.

MacTavish sighed. "Everything's a mess without Irene. She was here so briefly—but I came to rely on her like my right-hand man. Chong—could you get us some more moonsh—I mean, sterilization fluid?" The nurse nodded and waddled off.

"Is this, uh . . ." Jonah didn't know how to ask. He had chosen to stay behind when the others left, despite everything Irene had told him and the things he had heard with his own ears. He wasn't sure what to believe anymore, except that Dr. Slattery and his brother really did have Novo Mundum's best interests at heart. Some of the things they were doing were horrible, but it was to save them all.

Still—if he had a choice, Jonah wouldn't *personally* want to volunteer for the doctor's experiments on Strain 8 vaccines. . . .

Dr. MacTavish gave him a funny look. He panicked—was she going to tell Dr. Slattery about his suspiciousness? Wait, she didn't even *like* Dr. Slattery. What was she thinking?

"It's a real vaccine, as far as I can tell," she finally said quietly, squeezing his hand. Then the moment was over and Nurse Chong came back with an old-fashioned glass lab bottle with a sandblasted top and what looked like a wine pourer sticking out of it. "Ah, great, we can proceed."

He pulled up his sleeve and tensed his arm, remembering seeing kids do that in high school—but not for vaccines. Had they ever thought about it, the split-second decision that could have prevented them from getting AIDS, or tetanus, or high?

Whoa—how long had it been since the last time he let himself think about his old life, the way the world used to be? He hadn't even had one of those nightmares about his dad in *weeks,* maybe over a month. It was all Novo Mundum now. *Safe.*

Jonah flinched as the needle went in but didn't say anything.

SIX

KEELY SCRAPED HER HAIR BACK INTO A PONYTAIL, CHECKED IT in the mirror, then yanked the hair band out again. Nothing looked right.

"What, are you nervous?" Michael asked Keely as they all got ready to go out. They hadn't bothered waiting for her mom on the first night—even with whatever people in high places her mom knew, there was no way she would be able to get everything together so quickly. Now it was Friday and there was a strange excitement in the air beyond just that of meeting Keely's mother. Everyone was taking a little extra care in dressing: Diego had taken a pair of scissors and managed to butcher his hair into some kind of shape; Irene was putting on makeup. There was almost a *Friday night* thing going on.

"Sorry I'm late." Liza pushed the door open and barreled in, depositing a tote of groceries on the table. Cornmeal, a few ration bars, *eggs* . . . "They needed help doing inventory control at this community warehouse down the street. And if there's one thing Novo Mundum drilled into me, it was inventory and supply. So I got a quick job. They gave me some coupons in return."

"Good for you!" Michael hoisted a sack of cornmeal. "I'm impressed."

"Really," Keely said. "There are a couple of meals here. Thanks, Liza." Keely had once worried that Liza would be a serious liability to their escape, and with Michael's depression it had been hard going there for a while. But Liza was stepping up. Growing up, just as they'd all had to do.

Liza looked around, noticing that everyone else was ready to go. "Let me just go wash my face."

Keely turned to the mirror and scraped back her hair again.

"Third time's the charm?" Michael teased.

"Yeah, I'm nervous," Keely admitted. "I feel like she's going to ground me or something. I *left home*—it's like a divorce, sort of."

Outside, her spirits lifted a little, drawn from worry to wonder. It was only an hour before curfew, but the streets were packed with people taking a stroll—couples holding hands, families with little kids all cleaned up for the walk—and an early setting sun bathed everything in red excitement. The night air was balmy, with a hint of cooler weather that set the Texans readjusting their dusters, shawls, and jackets. Street vendors—studiously ignored by the soldiers—sold spiced pumpkin seeds and other, less identifiable snacks. A surprising number of cafés and restaurants were open.

Irene's eyes were shining; she and Diego were holding hands and looking out over the crowd. Yep, *très* romantic. A stab of self-pity struck Keely, different from her usual depression about Eric and Gabe: she was the odd man out in this party.

Irene was whispering something into Diego's ear and he laughed.

"Hey, we don't all have to go," Keely said gamely. "If you two want to have a night to yourselves or something."

"Are you sure?" Irene asked, kind and concerned as ever—but there was a gleam in her eye that said she and Diego were already gone.

"Yeah, go ahead," Keely said emphatically. As they promised they wouldn't be back too late and wandered off into the night, she knew they deserved it. They *all* deserved a night off, from traveling and hiding and being shot at and almost being injected with lethal viruses and freezing to death. . . .

"You can go too if you want," Keely said to the remaining couple. "I think I can face my own mom alone."

Liza turned to Michael and shrugged.

"No way." Michael shook his head. "Even if it wasn't

your mom we worried about, there could be people with her. We'll watch from a hidden position to make sure no one's with her before you go—and no one's following her while you're there."

"He's right," Liza agreed. "We should consider every possible scenario."

Just then a shot went off behind them.

The three whirled, Michael pulling Liza to the pavement beside him. Keely found herself ducking for cover, low to the ground, diving behind a steel lamppost. Amazing the instinct to duck for cover, drop out of sight, even before she could determine what was going on.

She found herself expecting the worst . . . a scream and a second shot. A body dropping in the crowd, the soldiers appearing with tear gas.

Instead she saw that someone was standing on an old oil drum, whooping and waving a poster of MacCauley, TOGETHER WE'RE STRONG emblazoned in red across the bottom. Someone else was taking very good aim and firing precisely into the words.

"*Texas* is strong!" the man shouted, waving his hat. Everyone whooped and cheered.

Keely felt herself breathe again, her heart thudding in recovery. *Just another protest. Texas style.*

"Oh my God," Michael whispered.

"Are they *insane?*" Liza demanded, hands still to her ears. She hadn't had quite as much experience with firearms as Keely or Michael. *Lucky girl.*

Taking their time, almost as if they were letting the crowd disperse on their own, soldiers came strolling over to confiscate the gun and break up the scene. Soon the demonstration was over, the crowd on the plaza milling around casually as if nothing had happened, the shooter laughing with his friends. That was the most surprising part to Keely: an outburst like this would not have been tolerated back in Los Angeles. At the very least, the man with the gun would have been hauled off and jailed. If it weren't for the slight smell of gun smoke, Keely would have questioned whether anything had really happened.

The three moved on, still shaken more than the locals.

"Can you believe what the soldiers allow here?" Michael said under his breath. "Whip out a gun in New York and they'd lock you up, along with half of the crowd. I guess we're just in the Wild West."

"They were pretty strict in L.A., too," Keely said, wondering if the government was beginning to soften. "You know, it's funny. When I lived in L.A., I never thought of anything changing. Life sucked, the government sucked, school sucked—you know, life as usual. Like everyone else, I was depressed about the deaths in my family, of my boyfriend, and couldn't look beyond that and how much life sucked."

"Well, after Strain 7 everything *did* suck," Michael pointed out. "And high school always sucked, even before."

"No, wait, listen." Keely took a deep breath. "When Novo Mundum contacted me, I thought I was saved. That my sucky life was over and I was going to my happily ever after. Which it was, sort of," she added apologetically to Liza.

"It was paradise city," Liza said. "I grew up and spent my entire life there. When Strain 7 happened and Daddy formed the community, it just seemed natural. . . . And we were still safe and happy, far away from everything else."

"That's my point," Keely said. "All of us were taking for granted that we basically lived under a crazy, fascist government and that it made some sort of sense because we had just undergone a huge national tragedy. None of us thought about *doing* anything about it."

"Like you think the people in Georgia are," Michael said slowly.

"And the people here obviously *want* to do something—they're just not sure how to go about it yet." Keely looked at the man on the barrel, holding the poster. His eyes were red, his jowls slack, probably from liquor. The man who'd shot the poster was smiling fiercely, angrily, calling after the soldiers who'd confiscated his gun. People were laughing and clapping him on the shoulder, but the moment was over and the crowd moved on, looking for the next spectacle.

"Something *does* need to be done," Michael agreed gently. "But right now we have—"

He paused, and Keely knew he was searching for a way to mention Liza's father without calling him a terrorist or a maniac or a homicidal lunatic.

"A man with the potential to unleash something worse than 7. Let's stop him first and *then* we can think about rebuilding America."

Keely gave him a grudging nod. She *hated* it—but he was right.

"There's the museum," Liza said. It was hard to miss, with giant cartoonish yellow pillars and the MUSEUM sign composed of large, friendly red letters. The building was dark and a couple of panes of glass had been smashed, but otherwise it wasn't too badly damaged. What looked like paper dolls of kids held up the roof on one side.

"Hey . . ." Michael pointed to a short woman standing next to one of the brightly colored child statues, dwarfed by it.

Keely sucked in a breath at the sight of the familiar silhouette of the woman she knew so well. Even from a distance her posture and hair were unmistakable. "Mom . . ."

SEVEN

AMBER HIT THE SIDE OF HER MONITOR AND LET OUT A FRUS-
trated groan.

"Jane! The server's down again!" she yelled out into
the hall.

"Better be just a memory leak or something simple. If
those stupid mice have gotten into the cables again . . ."
Jane appeared at the door, red-faced and annoyed, frumpy
in the skirt and top she wore in an effort to project some
semblance of normal office life. "Use 192.168.345.124
locally for now—manually copy and paste any important
messages still on the server from Dr. Slattery or Frank or
whatever and send them on."

Amber groaned again but nodded. "Will do."

Actually, she and Jane had been getting along

surprisingly well—finally. She wasn't a complete gobo, just tense with her responsibilities, and afraid of screwing up, and worshipful of the two brothers—the last of which was pretty much the norm at Novo Mundum anyway. Amber still looked at all of Jane's outgoing mail—mostly icky lovesick letters to her husband, one to her mom letting her know she was still okay—but she was definitely innocent of any real nefarious deeds.

Of course, what the nefarious deeds were and *who* was guilty of them was now kind of up in the air. It was a shock that Dr. Slattery had turned out to be some sort of psycho mad scientist—assuming Keely and everyone was right—and that his brother was responsible for killing Gabe and almost Michael. . . . But there were a lot of unanswered questions about everything. Like who really called in MacCauley's soldiers and why? Why were they all being given vaccines for some sort of new kind of Strain 7 if Dr. Slattery had told them over and over again that they were all immune to the original one?

Of course, all these conspiracy theories kind of took a backseat to worrying about her friends. Dr. Slattery had said they were captured by the Slash and killed—mourning for Liza had sprung up campus-wide in the form of fasting and black tatters of cloth wrapped around the upper arm. Amber wore one too—but it was for Keely. And for show. She didn't believe a word that came out of the mouth of slimy and insane Dr. Slattery. No way would her friends have let themselves get captured.

On the other hand, just the other day she had seen Jane giving her weekly report to Frank, Slattery's brother—and he looked wasted. Literally. His eyes were red and covered in a fine netting of veins; his skin was sallow and hung loose; there was defeat in his eyes. He kind of looked like a zombie or a person whose soul had been sucked out. Amber knew he doted on his niece, Liza, but with her gone it was like he had lost all purpose and desire.

That made her worry. Whatever the truth was about what had happened to her friends, *he* didn't think it was good.

Amber took a deep breath and put a hand to her belly, which was rounding nicely. Soon her belly button would turn inside out, if it was anything like those books Irene had given her before she left. Amber wasn't used to worrying about people *or* trying to think through such complicated, paranoid thoughts about everyone around her. She wasn't used to worrying about anyone much besides herself and, at one time, her old boyfriend. . . . *Too bad one of the others didn't stay—someone besides Jonah.*

She sighed and began to bury herself in her work, another thing that was new to her. "Who's gonna cry for y'all, who's gonna cry over you," she sang to herself, opening up the folder that held the IMAP mail in stasis on a hard drive. She very carefully began to open each mail to copy and paste it and resend it again. "Who's gonna cry over you. . . . Tell me would they lie for you. . . ."

She stopped right as she was about to send, her sub-conscious suddenly realizing what the words she had just pasted actually *said*.

Valdez and Smith chosen for sample run. Mitchell is a great scout, but we need him for the later tests here. Left at 0300 hours today. Decided to use all four vials in case wind changes direction. Arrival at TET expected two days from now. Considering Mitchell, Abrams, Flood, and Noonan for mission upon success of this one immediately thereafter under Tabori. —Frank

Mission? Tests? Vials of what? When she looked at the list of e-mails back and forth between Frank and his brother, a lot of them had *October Project* in the message header.

Amber rubbed the spot on her arm where the needle had gone in and wondered what to do.

EIGHT

KEELY WAS ALREADY WALKING INTO THE SHADOWS OF THE MUSEUM as Michael called to her, assuring her that he and Liza would keep watch. She paused a few feet from her mother's back, unsure of what she was going to say, whether she could actually do this. Her heart skipped a beat and thudded into the next one, a strange new fear clamped on her throat.

"Mom . . . ?" she managed to breathe out.

The short woman in the out-of-place business suit turned and blinked. For a moment Keely was afraid she couldn't recognize her. *It's only been a few months— have I changed that much?*

"Oh my God, *Keely!*" Her mom ran forward and grabbed her daughter tightly to her chest, as best as she could with the height difference. *Hey, I must have actually grown an inch or so. . . .* But Keely was shocked out of her thoughts by the sound of her mom sobbing—something she hadn't heard since her dad had first come down with symptoms of Strain 7.

"Mom . . . ?" Keely asked, more gently this time.

"I've been so *worried.* . . ." This was the point in TV shows or movies when the mother would then stand back and slap the daughter or at least yell something like, "How could you *do* this to me!" But she just squeezed Keely tighter for a moment before letting her go, finally wiping her eyes. "You look good."

"That's kind of surprising, considering—" She bit back what she was about to say, about the Slash and the frost and the not really eating for the past few weeks. "Considering," she said again, shrugging. "Have you been—uh—followed?"

Dr. Gilmore raised an eyebrow, slowly reverting back to the Dr. Gilmore mom Keely was used to. "Meet me at this secret unspecified location? Every night at dusk? Am I being *followed?* You're quite the little secret agent now."

"It's kind of a long story. But look, let's get you settled, and . . ."

"Get me settled? Honey, I came to take you *home.*"

Keely took a deep breath. "I can't, Mom. Not now. Like I said, there's a long story, and I have to see it through to the end."

Liza watched over her mug of tea as Keely snuggled into the couch next to her mom. How weird to see any of the kids in this group with a parent, especially Keely, the strong-minded, wise one. Mrs.—no, *Dr.* Gilmore—was sitting up straight, like a grown-up, carefully stirring her own tea. As if she was used to tea in bags—as if it wasn't a luxury the people at Novo Mundum used and re-used so sparingly. At least Dr. Gilmore had been cooperative when they'd asked her to come back to the apartment. She'd even changed into pj's they'd found at the apartment, giving the girls a chance to innocuously check if she was bugged. So far, so good.

Now Dr. Gilmore was playing with a strand of Keely's hair and commenting on how she looked more and more like her dad every day. Liza turned away, trying to tamp down a pang of jealousy. She barely remembered her own mother, who died of cancer long before Strain 7. She'd never had any close female relatives, but the small, tender gesture reminded her of her uncle Frank, the way he used to tug on her pigtails when she was little.

"Maybe you wouldn't mind having a look at my leg, too, Dr. Gilmore," Diego offered politely. "Everyone else has."

Keely's mom laughed dryly. "I'm not that kind of doctor, Diego."

"Yeah, about that . . ." Michael prodded, giving Keely a look. She was obviously reluctant to "start" anything with her mom immediately, still basking in the happy reunion.

Keely sighed and sat up. "Mom?"

Dr. Gilmore took a deep breath and looked around the room, taking each one of them in before starting.

Liza set her jaw in annoyance. *I'll bet she thinks of us as just kids. I'll bet she's wondering why she should even bother explaining anything to us.*

"I wasn't treating emergency patients," she admitted slowly. "Though I'm kind of surprised that a smart girl like you didn't figure that out earlier," she added with a bit of a sting. The group braced for Keely's reaction.

Liza would have been all over her. She'd had her fill of being lied to by a parent who thought it was for her own good.

But Keely just locked her eyes on her mother. "It has something to do with your background as a virologist, doesn't it?" she prodded.

"I don't see how burdening you with top secret information has anything to do with bringing you home, or why you ran away, or who you all are, or what you've been doing for the past few months."

"It has everything to do with it, Dr. Gilmore," Michael cut in, using that powerful, in-control voice Liza found so sexy. Now she just hoped it worked. She had never noticed before the strange position he was in, no longer a teenager and not an adult, missing his chance to go to college, to go to business school, to enter the corporate world—to take a place in top management at his dad's global alarm and security company. *Type-A leader.* Liza had loved that about him back in Novo Mundum, when there were people who needed to be led. But now that the dynamic had changed, Liza had become acutely aware of Michael's weaknesses. The trip through the Big Empty had been an eye-opener, making

Liza wonder if she and Michael really belonged together. Back in Novo Mundum he had fit into her life perfectly, but here, in a world that seemed to change by the hour, sometimes by the minute, she wasn't so sure of anything.

"We'll explain everything as soon as you do," Michael went on. "We'll tell you why we called you."

Dr. Gilmore was silent for a moment, fixing her steely light blue eyes on Michael's brown ones. "Strain 7 was a deadly fluke—which our government doesn't want to happen again. An insane amount of resources are being put into viral research right now. Everyone in the field left alive is in two facilities, one on the East Coast and one on the West. And they're both under heavy army supervision."

Everyone was silent as the words settled in. *Wow, we both have parents with hidden agendas.* Liza looked at Keely to see how she was taking this.

"Mom—why didn't you tell me?" Keely whispered.

"Because it's top secret—or didn't you hear that part?" her mom said, a little archly.

"*Why* are you doing this?" Michael demanded. "You and the government."

"I think I've told you just about enough for your purposes and far more than I should have," Dr. Gilmore said firmly. Liza could almost hear the *kiddo* at the end of it. "Now it's your turn."

"I think we're going to need a few minutes to talk about this," Irene suggested.

"What are you all?" Keely's mom demanded with

the faintest trace of humor. "Some kind of cult?"

"We were," Keely said, a little sadly. "Not anymore. That's why we needed to call you."

"Keely, you mind taking a time-out on this one?" Michael asked gently. He probably wanted her to keep her emotional response out of it.

"Me too," Liza found herself saying. "Political discussions bore me." Besides, she was a little sick of having her opinion discounted because she didn't share the same social background. Did they treat her like a bubble girl just because she had grown up on a college campus? Or was it the fact that her father had been plotting to wipe out thousands of people to protect his own?

"Liza can help me fill Mom in on the background of—*NM*." Keely caught herself quickly. "Up to the part before we left."

"Good idea." Michael nodded at Liza, as if entrusting her with the cure for Strain 7.

"Oh, goody." Liza stretched her legs, checking out the Gilmore girls. "I love a good story time."

NINE

CATHERINE GILMORE HAD A HARD TIME LISTENING TO THE story that the girl—Liza—was unfolding before her. Secret community? Didn't the government wipe them all out? The way she described it, the place sounded like a little pocket of hippie heaven in a depressing, rigidly controlled world. They grew their own food, harnessed solar power, encouraged arts and literature, fostered a sense of brother- and sisterhood that was lacking in the everyone-for-him-or-herself feeling that pervaded the cities where those exiled from the Big Empty had been shipped.

She had recognized some of that hardness in Michael's eyes—the one member of the group who had existed in the world as a near-adult. He had a little bit of that feral urban quality that too many people had these days. A place like "NM" should have softened it some.

Liza seemed to be his direct opposite, having grown up in a safe, academic community and continued to exist in a protected, golden world. Whatever the group had gone through in the last few weeks had obviously taken a toll on Liza, but she'd managed to keep an openness, a youthful innocence Dr. Gilmore's own daughter seemed to lack now.

Dr. Gilmore forced herself not to get melancholy. *If I had known Keely had run away to a place like NM, I wouldn't have worried so much.* In the end, it probably would have been better for her daughter if she had stayed there—assuming the government didn't find them.

They had no idea what this world was really like. Even Keely had no idea how bad things really were. How bad things could really get.

She shuddered, brushing away the cold, the worry that things would slow down without her there. Sanjay knew what he was doing; he had been postdoc when everything went down. Things would be fine. Really. Progress would be made.

Because every second they weren't working . . .

"Yeah," Keely was saying, "the work hours were really reasonable. Dr. Slattery did a great job of—"

"Dr. *Slattery?*" Dr. Gilmore suddenly interrupted. She must have heard wrong. "Dr. *Paul* Slattery?"

"Yeah," Liza said, surprised. Keely flushed with

embarrassment that she had let the name slip. "He's my dad. How do you know him?"

Catherine Gilmore didn't believe in coincidences or synchronicity. Suddenly she began to understand why they might have wanted to call her. . . .

"He's one of the country's top viral researchers. His papers are standard—*were* standard reading. We met at all these different protein conferences. . . . We even competed for the same consulting jobs for a while before he settled down at—where was it? Greenwich College? As their top-scientist-in-residence."

Liza was nodding at Keely. "Greenwich College. That's what was there before Novo Mundum."

"But Dr. Slattery . . ." Keely's mother pressed on. "I assumed he was dead from 7 after he didn't turn up at either of MacCauley's research facilities."

"Um, nope," Liza said uncertainly. She and Keely looked at each other—not sure why their information mattered.

But Catherine Gilmore was already connecting the dots, projecting scenarios, speculating. There was more going on here . . . much more.

TEN

"OKAY," MICHAEL SAID, SETTLING DOWN INTO THE CHAIR across from Keely's mom. Diego and Irene sat on either side of him, flanking him like officials, rather than sitting together the way they usually did. Smart. He really liked them as a couple—good, intelligent people whose talents were perfectly matched: Irene's book-learned knowledge of the world of humans and Diego's survival instinct and abilities. They were made for each other.

Michael wished he could say that about Liza and him. They were barely on the same page most of the time and didn't share that weird mental communication *thing* that Irene and Diego had. Lately he'd begun to wonder why they were together. It had made sense when he was playing the hero card back in Novo Mundum, but so much had changed since then.

"Keely's mom knows my dad," Liza said, drawing him back into the moment.

Irene pressed her hands to her face, trying to take it all in.

"Small world," Keely said with a weak smile.

"All right. This might make things easier, actually," Michael decided. That was one of his talents—taking a new situation or a change of plans and rolling with it smoothly, quickly adjusting and adapting.

"Liza and Keely had just gotten to the point where the group of you arrived at Novo Mundum and were getting settled in," Dr. Gilmore said, setting her teacup down. "And I think I need to hear this."

"Okay. Well, this is where things begin to change. . . ."

As Michael told the rest of the story, he found himself censoring less and less and revealing more details than he'd planned. This was *Keely's mom,* not just some random outside person that they had contacted for help. She was steelier than her daughter, but the twitch of her lips was a familiar precursor to Keely's wide smile, and there were freckles hiding underneath foundation on the tip of her nose. Plus she was scary smart. In a way—like Keely—that Michael wasn't. Logic and equations and *things* about the universe and science, like the engineers who used to work for his dad.

He wished he could have met her in other circumstances, just as Keely's mom, but considering the situation, he decided to go with his gut instinct and trust her.

". . . and then Irene led us to this place, so here we are."

The room was silent. Dr. Gilmore's face was unreadable, though a little pale. Another difference between her and her daughter: you could always tell what Keely was feeling.

"The only thing I really understand about all this," she finally said, "is that Paul is working on a 'Strain 8.'"

"Yes," Michael said, nodding vigorously.

"To protect 'NM' somehow," she added.

"Or to develop vaccines in case a Strain 8 spontaneously occurs," Liza protested weakly, one last time. Everyone in the room shot her a look, Dr. Gilmore the harshest of all.

"Let me give you a lesson in viruses since your father obviously hasn't." Catherine Gilmore dunked her teaspoon back into the tea and took it out, holding it up for everyone to see. It was still steaming a little. "This, just hot water with some tannin in it from the tea, is enough to kill most viruses. Put it or boiling hot water on a sponge and clean your counters and you're done, at least as far as most viruses go. A little Clorox would take care of the rest. I can't speak for other germs. But let's say, for a moment, that we're dealing with a particularly hardy and nasty strain, and this didn't work." She let the tea fall back into her cup, then waved the spoon around and blew on it until it dried. "*This* would definitely kill them. Most viruses are extremely fragile and can't live outside the moist, organic substrate they thrive in. Meaning that when snot, spit, blood, ejaculate, or whatever else dries up, almost all viruses die. That's why you don't get herpes 2 from toilet seats."

Michael tried to keep his lips from curling in an embarrassed smile; everyone else was shifting in their seats or looking uncomfortable as Dr. Gilmore spoke.

"What does this have to do with my dad?" Liza asked, and Michael suspected she was miffed at being the one singled out for the lecture.

"Viruses are *fragile*," Keely's mom said, a little exasperated. "Most of the time. And more than that, mutations are usually *bad* for the thing that mutates. In the same way that most badly mutated animals don't get born but die in the womb—except for the occasional two-headed cow—most 'spontaneous' viral mutations are bad for the virus too, or at least not necessarily 'good' for them. It's rarer than you think for one kind of virus to spontaneously mutate into another one without complicated processes, like the avian flu that goes from bird to *pig* to human vectors. In other words, there is almost no chance of a *random* Strain 8 virus popping up.

"If he's doing research on it, your father is most certainly *creating* it. Probably as a weapon."

While it was the conclusion they had all come to—except for maybe Liza—it was chilling to hear it spoken aloud.

"He was always a little bit of a nutter," Dr. Gilmore continued on reminiscently, eyes glazed with memories of the past. "Boring us with his quant notions of social theory . . . but I never thought he was such a megalomaniac. Sorry," she added to Liza.

Liza nodded, but her eyes were full of tears.

"If that's what he's doing, he's extremely dangerous. That's why we called you," Michael said softly. "We didn't want to tell the government because there are a lot of innocent people who would die in a normal raid. But with you along, we can go back, maybe destroy the lab properly or at least get you his books so you can figure out exactly what he's doing."

"Are you insane?" Dr. Gilmore demanded, dropping her superior stance in surprise. "You all got out of there safely. I have my daughter back. End of story."

"But what about his research?" Irene asked, shocked by the doctor's response.

"Remember that part of viruses being fragile? If he's in some sort of isolated community in the middle of the Big Empty—I'm guessing near Greenwich College—it doesn't matter. It's not going anywhere. Even assuming he perfected his new killer strain. I'll alert people to keep an eye out for it—but if anything goes wrong, we're looking at more of a Jonestown than a Strain 7, I think."

Michael bit his lip. How could she talk that way? Hadn't Liza told her about all of the innocent people at NM? How could she be so cold? She got her daughter back, and that was it?

"If my dad really is creating it as a weapon, he needs to be stopped," Liza said, swiping a tear from one cheek with the back of her hand. "And I want to be the one who helps."

"You all are welcome to come back to L.A. with me,"

Dr. Gilmore offered. "I have strong connections in the army and the government. I can get you placed in nice schools—" Keely made a rude noise. "Or good jobs, extra rations . . . We could use more self-starting, intelligent young people." She was looking at them brightly, as if this was the best thing in the world—how could they *not* be interested?

Dr. Gilmore might be a consummate scientist and worker, Michael realized, but she was terrible at buttering people up.

"Mom, this is serious," Keely said in an authoritative voice.

"*I'm* serious. I'm sorry about what you went through—it sounds horrible," Dr. Gilmore said with genuine feeling. "But I'm taking Keely, and we're going home."

ELEVEN

IRENE WAS PLAYING AROUND WITH KEELY'S COMPUTER, BORED and going stir-crazy.

All the kids in the group were nuts with tension. Diego had stomped off not ten minutes before, muttering something about finding some work. Or food. Or something. The discussion—argument, really— with Keely's mom had been going on for several hours, but now it was just between the mother and daughter. And it wasn't really a discussion *or* an argument. It was a screaming match. Sometimes Keely's voice dropped into a daughter's whine or wheedle, and sometimes they had the same tone so close they were virtually indistinguishable. The same woman, split in two.

I wonder if we would have ended up like that if Mom had lived.

Irene could see both sides—as usual. They were just a group of teenagers who had been in a cult and then the wild and had a crazy story about a crazy man who was making viruses to destroy the world. Or something. Meanwhile, Dr. Gilmore had *flown* all the way from L.A. to pick up her daughter and bring her home, she thought. Relief and joy at seeing her quickly became disappointment and anger when there turned out to be another agenda—and something she hadn't witnessed herself.

After twiddling her thumbs and pacing the apartment for a while Irene had finally approached the laptop, battered and scratched from their journey—but surprisingly not waterlogged. It was a sign of just how barbaric and regressive the Slash were that they hadn't recognized its worth or bothered to confiscate it. Frankly, it was a miracle that it had made the trip intact—Keely had set it up first thing, plugging it in to charge and giving it a simple diagnostic, and it was fine. Except for the N key, which had popped off somewhere along the line.

Searching around the desktop, Irene found solitaire and began to play it. Surfing the web would have been better—Keely and Michael had it all set up for wireless something or other, but she was afraid of screwing something up, of somehow alerting the world to their presence.

Michael paced nervously in front of the bedroom that Keely and her mom were in, listening at the door occasionally.

"She *has* to help us," he muttered. "What else are we going to do?"

"I don't know," Liza said, shrugging. She was flipping through an old *Vogue,* the kind that had eight hundred pages and weighed several pounds. She looked so natural doing it, Irene felt a pang. It was like a glimpse of the old days, a vision of the girl Liza might have become if it weren't for Strain 7. *Do they even print fashion magazines anymore?* Irene had never been a big fan, but she found herself missing a lot of things she'd never really liked, things that had meted out the rhythm and patterns of life before Strain 7.

"But if you haven't noticed, they're arguing," Liza added, eyes on the magazine. "I think you'd better come up with a plan B. One that doesn't involve Keely."

Irene looked at her, shocked. There was a *trace* of smugness on Liza's face, but it was like the memory of an old emotion. It was obvious she didn't envy or hate Keely as much as she used to. But she was right: tearing Keely away from her mom might not be so easy a second time.

On the other hand, from the way they're fighting . . .

"She'll do the right thing," Michael said, but it was unclear whether he meant the mother or daughter.

"Keely might, but Gilmore Senior can call up government army types to help her," Irene pointed out.

Suddenly there was a little sound that Irene hadn't heard in a long time—the chime that tinkles when you have a new e-mail. Curious, she flipped through the various windows that were open until she came to Outlook.

And there it was—a strange message highlighted in bold from vun@Moonmud.com. She opened it, relieved that it didn't tell her that the sender wanted a receipt.

Sticky stuck flies for ever
Eons on trees sap
The tub's Leeky:
How many weeks? Then will tell.

Irene's hand wavered over the delete key—this was the sort of thing that used to clog e-mail accounts, random words and phrases that helped slip them by spam catchers; usually further down in the message was an ad for something to enhance your sex life. Only this was a post–Strain 7 world, and there was nothing else in the message.

"Guys . . . ?" she said slowly. "Come take a look at this."

Michael reluctantly gave up his snooping at Keely's door and came over, obviously convinced it was something irrelevant. But his eyes widened when he saw the gibberish. "It looks like a code. Remember the messages we got from Novo Mundum? Back when we were in Clearwater?"

At the time Irene had been busy trying to save Diego's life, but she remembered some of the patterns—the anagrams and numeric substitution. "Get Keely," she said quietly. "She was the expert."

"Keely?" Michael shouted.

The door behind them opened slowly and Keely said in a carefully measured voice, "What?"

"I think you'd better see this." Michael pointed at the screen.

Keely frowned, pursing her lips. "Looks like gibberish—but there's only one word actually spelled wrong." Her eyes widened. "And *Leeky* is an anagram for *Keely.* And the sender . . . *vun at Moonmud* . . . it's *Novo Mundum,* with the letters rearranged!"

"Yeah, but 'sticky stuck flies forever'?" Michael prodded grimly. "It's going to take days to figure out what that's an anagram for."

"No, dummy," Keely said excitedly, pressing closer to the keyboard. Irene gave up her seat, deferring to the expert. "Flies get stuck in tree sap, which turns into *amber* over millions of years. Get it? Amber. She's sending us a note. The part I can't figure out is *How many weeks?* If this is an emergency message, shouldn't she be telling us something? In code but like directly?"

"Maybe it's some sort of check question to make sure the right people got it," Michael said. "But how many weeks what? We've been gone? We traveled together? We were there?"

"No." Irene spoke up. She couldn't do the word stuff, but the answer to this was obvious for anyone who really thought about Amber—or out of the box. "How many weeks she's been *pregnant.*"

Michael and Keely stared at her without congratulating her. Waiting, almost. *What are they . . . ? Oh.* "It's twenty-four."

Keely began typing as soon as the words were out of Irene's mouth.

"Good job," Michael said, giving her a pat on the back. It was foolish, but Irene couldn't help feeling a little surge of pride. A small thing, but she'd contributed.

24. what up?

"How did Amber know where to send it?" Irene ventured.

"This was originally her computer," Keely said, hitting send. "Or actually, Faith Stank's computer. I'll bet that because she works with the computers now, she can send messages using whatever method Jane uses."

"I just hope she deletes them afterward," Michael muttered.

"What's going on?"

Dr. Gilmore strolled out of Keely's room, towel-drying her hair and wrapped in the previous occupant's robe. *For someone who seems so uptight and proper, she certainly adjusts quickly,* Irene noted. She couldn't imagine her own mom putting on a dead woman's bathrobe and casually hanging out with a bunch of teenagers she had just met. But Keely's mom almost seemed to be *enjoying* it a little. . . . Maybe those months by herself had made her realize how much she missed having people around her, a family.

"We got a message from one of our friends who stayed behind," Michael explained.

"Well, let me know if it's something important," Dr. Gilmore said casually, heading over to the stove to turn on the hot water.

Bad answer, Irene thought, noticing how Keely's face darkened with anger and Michael rolled his eyes. Surprising—after all they'd been through, Dr. Gilmore still didn't give them much credit.

Everyone jumped when the mail tone rang—even Dr. Gilmore.

Keely opened it:

Plans for testing codenamed doublebush under October project releasing it everywhere—killzone?
EVERYONE HERE INJECTED

TWELVE

DIEGO STRODE DOWN THE STREET, FORCING HIS WEAK LEG TO work, realizing that exercise was the only way it was going to get better. If he still lived by himself in the woods, the wound would have been fatal. Even if he hadn't died of an infection, he might have died of dehydration while recovering, unable to walk.

Instead Irene had saved his life and turned things upside down. He was still hiding from the government, but add to that injection with some horrible disease by a mad scientist, torture by the Slash, and adjustment to this overburdened Texas city in the Occupied Zone. No world was safe, but it was definitely an easier fight when he was with Irene.

Diego sighed, indulging himself in the small fantasy

that kept him going when he felt like giving up—Irene and him living in his old cabin, just the two of them, with some gardens and the game that he got, maybe a few chickens if he could find them. She wasn't the type of girl who would shirk hard work—and she could teach the kids everything he couldn't. Academic stuff.

Diego paused, looking around at the people moving beside and past him, more in a few blocks than were in all of Novo Mundum. All grit-jawed and serious about something—survival, getting through the day without attracting the soldiers' attention, a chance to bring home a few chocolate bars for the family. He had been seduced by that concept in Novo Mundum, for the first time in his life surrounded by people, all of whom were dedicated to the task of building a new society—one that even his nonnie might have approved of. And while what they'd found out had become a major disappointment, Diego couldn't let go of that idea of a community, the warmth of friendly people around him.

He would never admit it to anyone, but it would be hard to go back to living completely alone—even with Irene.

A small crowd had gathered near a hot dog stand that had been converted into a shoe repair shop. The owner had the volume on his world band radio turned as high as it would go and was listening to it with an ear pressed to the speaker, occasionally relaying to those around him what was being said. One woman turned and walked away, tears streaming down her scrunched-up face; others just shook their heads.

"What's going on?" Diego asked the man standing next to him. Unlike Liza, Keely, Irene, and Michael, he didn't stand out in the crowd—especially in Texas. His accent was soft, a mix of southern and south-of-the-border. Between that and his general politeness he fit in just fine.

The man barely gave him a look-over before responding. He was in his thirties, tan, with creases in his face that were still a little pale. The way he stood, the way he tucked in his shirt, the slight flab around his gut, he looked like someone who had been forced to start working outside after a life sitting in front of computer screens.

"There's this crazy peacenik hippie community north of here, kinda like Red Haven. . . ."

Diego's stomach froze and he found himself going completely still, the way he would in the woods, terrified he had made a noise that would frighten the game away. *He couldn't mean . . .*

"Some people trade with them—they're harmless." The man shrugged. "No one's heard from them in a few days, and now there's a government report coming through that they're all dead."

THIRTEEN

MAYBE I'M MISINTERPRETING THIS. I MUST BE . . . KEELY thought as she stared at the computer screen in horror. She huddled over the laptop with Michael and Liza, her mother hovering above them.

"That's one hell of a Jonestown," her mother muttered.

"Oh my God," Irene said, sucking in her breath. "He wouldn't do that—really? Would he? Kill everyone?"

Keely felt her eyes sting, but she fought tears. "It . . . fits the profile of a cult leader. Afraid of losing control, killing himself and all of his followers."

"How was he losing control?" Michael asked, his fists curling up.

"His daughter just ran away," Keely pointed out.

"Wait a second," Liza snapped. "I know you all think my dad's an insane—what do you call it? A megalomaniac, but whatever, he's not *that* insane. I can almost believe him hurting other people to save his own family and Novo Mundum—but he's not about to kill himself and all the people in his community."

"Well, you're reading it right there!" Michael snapped back, pointing at the screen. "In Amber's own words!"

"I can't believe it's true," Irene murmured, tears beginning to leak down her face.

Keely looked away from her, not wanting to see her pain, knowing it would make her break down and cry too.

"Why would Amber e-mail you just to let you know they were all going to die?" her mom asked suddenly. "Without, I mean, a cry for help, or a goodbye, or something? This seems like a pretty cold warning from someone who's just figured out she and everyone around her has a week to live."

Actually, it wasn't out of the realm of the possible for Amber, who *did* get matter-of-fact and cold at the most trying emotional moments. But her mom's point gave Keely pause. She thought about the two messages: if it was just an announcement of everyone at Novo Mundum's imminent death, why *would* Amber go to the trouble of a coded statement to make sure it was them? Something wasn't adding up.

"She's right," Keely said aloud. "If Amber was afraid of being caught, wouldn't she just send out a warning?

Why all the cloak-and-dagger, making sure we had a secure communication line if she was going to be dead in a week?"

"Uncle Frank wouldn't let this happen," Liza protested weakly.

"Oh my God, my dad, Aaron . . ." Irene began to sob. Michael put a hand on her shoulder but looked questioningly at Keely. He suspected something too.

Then the door slammed open and Diego practically fell in. He was out of breath and red in the face, holding his bad leg up a little like a horse when it rests a foot.

"Have any of you heard of Twin Elms Two?" he demanded, making his way to the couch. Irene leapt up to help him, wiping at her tears. Keely shook her head and Michael shrugged.

"Twin Elms is one of the communities my dad was interested in," Liza said, surprising Keely. "It was a commune in Washington or something. He liked their work model. I've never heard of a second one, though."

"Diego," Irene began. "Something terrible has happened. . . ."

"Yeah, holy crow, they're all dead," Diego said, still huffing.

Everyone froze.

"At this Twin Elms Two, in north Texas," he went on, not understanding the looks on their faces.

Keely looked back at the computer. *Doublebush.* Twin Elms. "What are they dead of?"

Diego shrugged. "The only thing that anyone really knows is that they all seem to have dropped dead of some disease a lot like Strain 7. The army found out and put a blockade around the whole area—ten miles around. Apparently a regular trader went for a weekly pickup and found them all dead or dying—he panicked and called the government."

"Not unreasonable," Dr. Gilmore said, though she had a disgusted look on her face.

"There's practically panic in the streets." Diego jerked his thumb back toward the door. "Everyone thinks the government did it, or it's been sent by God to finish off everyone who's left, or whatever. Rumors are flying—but from what I've heard, the people had blackened skin and faces and were shriveled like from no water." He looked at them meaningfully.

"Strain 8." Irene said aloud what all of them were thinking. "The October Project."

"That's what the symptoms are," Keely explained to her mom. "Diego saw people who had been injected with it—guinea pigs. They all had blackened skin too."

"I knew it had to be developed to be a weapon," Dr. Gilmore said, nodding. "What else could it be?"

"Look." Keely pointed to the screen. *Plans for testing codenamed doublebush.*

"He tested it out on them first," Michael said at the same time she was thinking it. Kind of freaky, really, how much they thought alike. And how quickly. "To make sure it worked. A nice, isolated community like themselves—no real chance of spreading. Looks like it was a success," he added with bitter irony.

"What about the guy who found them all?" Liza asked.

"Oh, if he contacted the government about it, he's nice and locked up by now. Quarantined," Dr. Gilmore said with false cheeriness.

"So somehow they managed to inject everyone at Twin Elms Two with it?" Diego asked skeptically. "How do you manage that? In their sleep?"

"She doesn't say *they* were injected," Dr. Gilmore pointed out. "She said everyone *here* was injected—presumably NM or whatever."

"And she specifically says 'releasing it everywhere,'" Keely said. "Probably creating a 'killzone' around the area. 'Releasing it' sounds more like dispersion in the air or something."

"Okay," Irene said slowly. "So they dispersed Strain 8 all around Twin Elms Two, killing everyone. Like Dr. Slattery was testing it. All that makes sense." She covered up the first part of Amber's message with her hand now that they had figured it out. "But what about that last line—'everyone here injected'?"

Everyone stared at the computer, thinking quietly.

"She didn't say they had all been *infected*," Michael suddenly pointed out. "Just that they had been *injected*." He and Keely looked up at each other at the same time, the solution to the puzzle working itself out in the space between their eyes.

"So?" Diego prompted.

"So they were probably *inoculated*," Keely explained. She smiled grimly at Amber's note; clear communication was not one of the girl's talents. *What a horrible, horrible way to misread something.*

"In case the virus got out while they were testing it?" Diego asked. "So no one there would get hurt?"

"Not just while they were testing it—for the end goal," Dr. Gilmore said, nodding. "This was Slattery's plan all along."

"I don't get it," Irene said honestly, looking back and forth between Keely, her mom, and Michael.

"It's the perfect defense," Michael said, whistling. "With everyone at Novo Mundum safe and immune with the vaccine, he can release the virus into the environment—providing the community with much safer protection than an electric fence."

"Can you do that?" Diego asked. One of the things that Keely liked about him was how he never put himself down for something he didn't know. If he was curious, he asked.

"Absolutely. The government's been afraid of something like this for *years*," Dr. Gilmore answered. Everyone turned to face her, waiting for a full explanation. Keely tried not to grimace—she *hated* it when her mom lectured, but this was important. "In the sixties, afraid of biological warfare, the army released a minor stomach flu—mostly harmless—into the subway tunnels of New York to see how it would spread and where it would settle, in case anyone used a real nasty one. It was supposed to break down pretty rapidly—but the warm, moist environment of the tracks kept it around longer than it was supposed to. People were coming down with strange cases of 'food poisoning' and tummy bugs for weeks afterward."

"Well, I guess that answers that," Michael said.

"He really is insane," Dr. Gilmore murmured, staring at the screen but obviously not seeing it—the same look she'd had at home, before Keely left, when she sat in the living room and stared at the TV.

"It's only just around Novo Mundum," Liza said, shrugging. "No one lives around there. So what's the problem?"

"You don't know about that," Keely said. She turned to Michael. "Remember Jeremy?"

"You mean spooky boy?" Michael shivered, shaking his head.

Keely rolled her eyes. "We met him in a town of dead people on our scouting mission. He pretended his mom and dad were still alive and lived off of what he scavenged in the Wal-Mart. Who knows how many others like him managed to stay behind, to slip through the government's net as they hauled everyone out? Whole towns—like Twin Elms and Novo Mundum—managed to. Why can't there be more?"

"And if you're that intent on protecting yourself, you're not going to stop there," Michael said, nodding. "I just wanted an electric fence. Then Frank wanted a *lethal* electric fence. The term is *kill* zone. What will it be tomorrow if he and Paul suddenly get nervous about something else?"

"If he made a virus strong enough to encapsulate itself and remain inactive in the environment until a host comes along," Dr. Gilmore said slowly, "or one that can actually survive in its active form without humans, by itself, or in some other vector like mice or deer, there can be no 'boundaries.' It may start at just a few miles around, but the rivers he dumps it into will empty out somewhere, the water will drain into the earth, the silt will wash somewhere else—hell, a good *storm* could blow the little bastards hundreds of miles away."

"I thought you said viruses were delicate," Liza said.

"I didn't think your father was this good," Dr. Gilmore admitted.

"He could start a whole new plague." Irene ran her fingers through her hair, showing just a little of the old Strain 7 panic, the fear of those still living in the middle of it that you could get it anywhere—from anything—and wind up like those around you, dead in the streets.

"*Now* will you help us?" Michael asked, turning to Keely's mom.

"I don't think I have much of a choice," she answered grimly.

FOURTEEN

"I CAN'T BELIEVE WE'RE GOING BACK," IRENE SAID, LOOKING AT the sky to the north. She and Diego sat on a bench in one of Houston's tiny corner parks and watched the sun set, red and huge. There was a strange metallic taste in the air; everything felt like the end of the world.

"I know." Diego took her hand in his and kissed her lightly on the cheek.

"Why does it have to be us?" she asked stubbornly, louder. But her voice was muted by the dry winter air. "We just *escaped* from that place. Now we have to return to what might be a place saturated with a deadly disease, a place full of people who probably hate us and a man who wants us dead? I don't mean to sound selfish, but haven't we been through enough?"

"Do you see Superman anywhere?" Diego asked, his dark eyes skimming the horizon lazily. When they were alone, he was able to switch gears, assuming a reckless, bad boy persona that didn't take the world too seriously. "No? Then it really is just us. And while I might have my reservations about sticking my neck out for a whole bunch of people who never did anything good for me, there's a lot of other people out there who have already been through enough."

"I know." Irene leaned against him, her head against his shoulder, wishing she could absorb some of his resolve. "We're lucky to even be alive at this point. We should pass that on. It's a mitzvah."

Diego raised an eyebrow at her.

"Good deed," she translated, smiling gently. "Doing something for others. It's a pretty big part of Judaism, at least the way I was raised."

They were quiet for a moment; she could feel him looking down at her, studying her face.

"What's really the problem?" he asked softly. "You're a brave girl, Irene. And you were going to dedicate your life to saving people. I know you're tired, but this doesn't really sound like you."

Irene blinked, trying not to cry. He knew her so well—already, so quickly.

"You're afraid of seeing your dad again, aren't you?" he whispered, stroking her hair.

She nodded. "Sort of. Afraid of his anger over our escape. Dreading his disappointment when he learns what Dr. Slattery is really about. I've been putting all these feelings off, thinking I wouldn't see him for a while."

"But now that's changed," Diego said. "After you went through so much to break with your dad and brother. Hey, I know it was a huge deal."

She nodded, swallowing hard. Her dad had gone through so much to bring them to Novo Mundum, where he really believed they would be safe and could grow up away from the government, free to be what they wanted. Her dad had embraced the notion of this utopian society; he'd bought the whole package.

Irene still remembered the anger on her father's face when she'd suggested that maybe something wasn't quite right at Novo Mundum, that Dr. Slattery wasn't the pure leader and savior everyone there thought he was. He probably considered it a complete betrayal that she left.

"He's going to hate me," she whispered, not wanting to say the words too loudly, in case it made them true.

"No, he won't. Look at Keely and her mom. Now, *there's* a screwed-up parent-child relationship if I've ever seen one." He grinned and touched the tip of her nose. "Keely left her mom the same way you did your dad—and they're finding their way back to each other. If they can, so can you two. Your dad *loves* you, Irene. More than Novo Mundum."

He gave her a squeeze and kissed her briefly on the

lips. Maybe he was right. But then, he didn't really know her father. She wasn't sure she did, either.

"I just don't know what we're going to do once we're there—we have to come up with a plan," Michael said, pacing back and forth in the bedroom Liza shared with Keely.

Michael and Liza were alone in the apartment, laying out the things they thought would be necessary for the trip. First-aid kit, check. Toothbrush—funny, really, but check. He paced to the window, taking in the flat, low buildings that stretched out along the horizon. "Never thought I'd say this, but I'm going to miss Houston."

Liza was stretched out on the bed, leaning on one elbow as she stared at an old catalog. "At least Dr. Gilmore will make this trip easier. She says we're riding on a train."

Michael stared at her, at the way she flipped the pages with disinterest. Much as he dreaded this trip, it couldn't be easy for her. "It's going to be tough going back for you, isn't it?"

She tossed the question back to him. "What's it like for you?"

Michael stopped in the middle of folding a T-shirt. "What?"

"Drop the man-in-control thing for a minute," she ordered. "What's going on in your head?"

"In my head?" Michael paused in front of the mirror, intrigued by her question. "I guess my head is always on the next angle, the next plan. Strategy as a means of survival." After Strain 7 he'd managed well in New York by playing the angles. But he was a wanted felon in that city, thanks to his idiot girlfriend Maggie. And while it was his decision to take her and *go*, save her from the government, the result was their wandering aimlessly in the Big Empty. Then he had found Novo Mundum and thought he had a place to stay. He fit in and Dr. Slattery liked him. He had a life, a job, an ambition, and a girlfriend again. Then he had to leave what seemed like a paradise because of the snake that ran it, because a friend had been killed and more killings had been planned.

And just when he was getting used to being back in civilization, feeling it slip on again as comfortable as an old coat, they had to pack up and head back into the Big Empty.

"So . . ." Liza persisted. "How do you feel about going back?"

"The truth? I'd be happy never to step over the line into the Big Empty again." He threw the T-shirt down on the floor. "I don't function well outside the loop, outside the society I know. You know, after Strain 7, New York was insane, but I did okay with it. I was able to adjust, work the connections we had. I helped my father forge on with his company—even lined up some new contacts. And the rest of it . . ." He shrugged. "Somehow it just worked for me; the coupons and curfews were not an issue. I could barter my way to a great cup of coffee or convince the soldiers in the street to extend the curfew for me." He felt a catch in his chest, thinking back on those days with an odd fondness.

Liza sat up and crossed her legs. "You make it sound sort of fun."

"It was all very do-able." A much easier life than he'd realized at the time, but then, you always kicked yourself over those things after the fact. "Not anymore."

"Come on, Michael." Liza folded her arms. "You're a flexible guy. Look at everything you've adapted to."

He shook his head. "Diego's the guy who can live by himself and survive happily in the wilderness. I need roots, a society where I can figure out the rules and ways to bend them. I thrive on the networking thing, which is one of the reasons NM worked for me. But once we get back there, if we're successful, there won't be a Novo Mundum. And although I know that's necessary, it goes against my grain to destroy a society that works."

It was weird letting it all out. These were tiny thoughts that had been niggling at the back of his brain ever since the first waves of Maggie-inspired heroism had begun to wear off. He had ignored them, but they had remained, quiet, underneath. And here he was, spilling them all out to the one person in the group who needed to hear it the least, who *needed* someone to depend on, who needed a hero.

"You know what?" she said. "After all that, you never even answered my question. How do you feel about going back to Novo Mundum?"

He sank onto the bed beside her. "I dread it."

He let his chin drop down, surprised to feel Liza's hand touch his shoulder.

They were alone in the apartment, a perfect opportunity to get horizontal, but neither of them seemed interested in that part of their relationship anymore.

She squeezed his shoulder reassuringly. "I appreciate everything you've done for me," she said. "Whatever happens between us, I just wanted you to know that."

When he looked up, her face seemed confident and calm, as if she'd discovered a distant peace and was already halfway there in her mind. "I'll always be there for you," he said.

She nodded. "I know that." She let her hand drop from his shoulder, then made a fist and fake-punched the side of his jaw. "Like the brother I never had."

"If that's what you want."

She let out a breath. "You know me—never really sure what I want. But right now, let's just say a plan to infiltrate Novo Mundum is at the top of my list too."

Michael nodded. "Then we'd better get working on that."

Keely leaned into the mirror, pulling her lips back and looking at her teeth. She had brushed and flossed as soon as they had settled into Irene's aunt's place. If there had been mouthwash, she would have used that too. It looked like she had gotten most of the tartar off, but her back molars still felt a little fuzzy. This would be the last time in a while when she could do anything even slightly dental. Keely sighed and slid the tooth-paste into a plastic bag, the closest thing she had for a cap.

"When this is all over," her mom said from behind her, and then stopped, as if she didn't know what to say. "When this is all over, will you come back home with me?"

"I don't know, Mom," Keely said, looking down at the precise moment her mother looked up. Their gaze never met in the mirror. "I don't even know *how* it's 'all going to be over.'" She threw a few more toiletries into her bag, the bare minimum. At the bottom was the lip-stick she had taken from the mall, the MAC Viva Glam she used to wear all the time. Keely smiled sadly as she zipped up the case.

"What's that supposed to mean?" her mother asked, forcing cheer. "I'm sure it will all work out all right."

Keely swung around and finally met her mother's eyes, fixing her with a glare.

"Okay . . . that sounded lame," her mother admit-ted, sighing, sitting back on the bed. "At one time you never *could* have imagined that there was a chance that something you chose to do could result in your own death. Or your mother's. Or everyone around you."

She didn't say it accusatorily; she said it wearily. For some reason, that was far worse.

"You've changed," she added, in a curious voice.

"I haven't changed *that much*, Mom," Keely said, sit-ting heavily down on the bed next to her. This was the conversation she didn't want to be dragged into. *How could it be that you faced down starving, freezing, homicidal maniacs, loaded guns, the threat of being made into a sex slave—and your mom could* still *accuse you of growing up without her permission?* "I hated the system back home. I skipped school whenever I could."

"And you, the National Honor Society student!"

"That life is over, Mom. You know that," Keely said quietly. "It ended the same day you had to start lying to me about what you did every day."

Her mom looked down at the carpet and pointed her toes, as if that was the interesting thing she was noticing.

"Remember September 11? Everyone thought it was the end of the world. Boy, were we all wrong. 'Some say the world will end in fire . . .'"

". . . 'some say in ice,'" Keely finished, smiling. It had been her favorite poem in eighth grade. Robert Frost.

"Instead it's disease, fatalism, atrophying of the American spirit."

"It doesn't have to be that way," Keely said firmly, thinking about the protest and riots. "There is no reason that over two hundred years of freedom should end in two of misery. The protesters in Georgia, the people we saw on the street the other night . . ."

"Keely, what can we do? What can *you* do?" her mother asked, waving her hand around, indicating the five who had come back from Novo Mundum. "Your friend Michael may be a little full of himself, but he didn't have the wrong idea—trying to make a life in this world."

"If no one thinks they can do anything, nothing will

change," Keely said, setting her jaw. "You never taught me to be a coward."

Her mother looked at her and Keely had the intense urge to look away, but she held her gaze. "We can make a difference," Keely said.

Catherine Gilmore pressed her lips together, nodding. "I hope you're right, honey. God, I hope you're right."

FIFTEEN

LIZA WATCHED AS THE REST OF THE GROUP SETTLED INTO THE train seats. They weren't giddy to the point of having to repress giggles, but everyone seemed to like his or her new status as official government passenger just fine. Liza had never been on a train before—planes and cars, yes, but never a train or a bus. It was a strange mix of communal and private passage: while they had this one car more or less to themselves, unless you sat at one of the center groups of seats that faced each other around a table, you sat in pairs of seats, two by two, that looked into the back of the seat in front of you.

She couldn't imagine being forced to travel long distances like this—what if you got sat next to some skanky guy or fat, insane woman?

"I don't remember a working Amtrak station when we came through St. Louis," Michael muttered, settling in next to Keely.

"This is mainly for moving troops," Dr. Gilmore said, pointing out the window at the uniformed men and women who made up most of the waiting passengers. "And government officials in charge of evacuating the Big Empty."

Everyone quieted when the car doors opened and a new group of passengers boarded, civilians, sleek and important with expensive clothes and heavy laughs.

"Bear season used to be *over* by now, remember?" one of them said with an ironic chuckle.

"Last two weeks before Thanksgiving. Don't remind me. Like you had a chance to *see* one in that time!"

As they passed by in the aisles, it was more than obvious that they were unencumbered by any luggage—these weren't the kind of people who carried their own. A few had expensive-looking rifles, however, in leather slings across their backs.

As soon as they were out the other door, Michael turned in his seat to look back at Keely's mom.

"*Troop* movements, huh?" he asked, a little bitterly.

"And you thought all the looting was done by kids on the street." The older woman sighed. "A lot of people—friends of friends of the government—get special privileges even in this new world order. I know a certain ex-governor of California who sort of, uh, *owns* Tahoe now."

"Do you get any 'special privileges'?"

"We're here, aren't we?" Dr. Gilmore snapped, turning back to the book she had found.

"Oh my God, remember the cheese trays?" Keely said, sighing. "I used to get those whenever we took the train to Oceanside to surf."

"I was mainly MTA or Metro North," Michael said, slipping into the seat across from her. "They sold exactly jack for food. And don't even ask about the bathrooms."

"Look what Keel's mom had!" Irene said excitedly, shaking a small pack of something in her hands. *Cigarettes?* That would be so unlike her. . . .

"Oh my God, deal 'em," Michael said, rubbing his hands together. "Poker? Bridge?"

"Hearts?" Keely countered.

"I only know gin rummy and go fish," Irene apologized. As she began to deal the cards and the three of them argued over what to play, Liza noticed that—just for a fraction of a day, these twenty minutes here—everyone was as happy as on a sitcom. A lot of it was forced because they couldn't actually *do* anything until they got back to Novo Mundum. Michael was convinced there might be bugs in the cars, and the occasional march-through of MacCauley-style soldiers with grim faces and big guns didn't allow them to make plans aloud. So there was nothing else to do but enjoy the trip.

"This seat taken?" Diego asked suddenly from above her. He had a hot cup of tea and a smile.

"It is now," Liza said, scooting over. Whatever they'd

had on the trip away from Novo Mundum had been gone since they were in Houston—and not just because it was obvious he and Irene were back together again, if they were ever really apart. While she was suddenly nervous, Liza was glad he was taking time out to talk to her.

"Here, you want this?" He held up the cup and she took it, although too late she realized he didn't have any packets of sugar or anything. Liza *hated* tea without some sort of sweetener. But she didn't say anything.

"Thanks," she said, forcing herself to sip it.

"I didn't want it. Just an excuse to get up and move around the train—explore it. No café car, but there's a couple of coffee and hot water dispensers." He pushed a button and stretched back so the seat reclined, grunting in pleasure as he stuck out his healing leg. She hadn't even known the seats did that. "I took a train a couple of times when I was growing up, mainly to see Nonnie," he said dreamily, looking out the window. "The trip took a whole day—Mom and Dad didn't trust buses. I kept my face pressed up against the window the entire time—I couldn't *believe* all of that land—all that nature out there. It was like a whole world without people."

"You've never liked crowds much, huh?" Liza said with a faint smile. "You must have *loved* Houston."

His face darkened, and for a moment Liza worried that she had screwed up their one chance to talk.

Diego saw her reaction and his face softened. "It sucked," he admitted quietly. "That was my idea of hell back there—thousands of people, *millions* of people, I can't even imagine—with nothing to do, no hope, no future. I gotta tell you, I thought about taking off a few times back there."

Liza's jaw dropped. How close had Diego come to leaving? "How could you even *think* it?" she demanded before she could stop herself.

"Don't think I'm not grateful for the whole saving-my-life-after-I-was-shot thing," Diego said with a chuckle. "Since I've been with you guys, I've been forced to join a crazy cult, *not* had my leg fixed, almost been injected with a deadly disease—seen people injected with this deadly disease—forced to escape this crazy cult, lead a bunch of tenderfoots through one of the worst early winter storms I've ever seen, and gotten shot at by someone who was supposedly my friend. I've gone hungry, cold, wet, tired, been caught and tortured by the Slash, escaped them only because the whim of one complete nutter butter of a girl, made to go to a city—*stay* in the city—and told I have to go back and maybe do it all over again. For the good of a world I'm not really sure I care about."

Liza opened her mouth, not sure how to respond to his rapid-fire list of complaints. "Well, when you put it that way . . ."

Diego shot her a cynical smile. "Don't think I'm complaining. This whole thing has changed us all, in different ways, and I'm glad for that. Glad to have hooked up with some people I care about."

Liza knew that "some people" equaled Irene. He

watched as she covered her eyes with embarrassment, having just made a bad play in the card game.

Liza felt a tug of jealousy. That was the kind of relationship she wanted, a solid connection, a lasting love. Maybe that was why she'd admired Diego in the first place—because of his strong attachment and loyalty to Irene. She'd tried so hard to create that sort of bond with Michael, but wishing couldn't make that happen.

Which led her to the big thought bubble. Michael. They had to talk.

"It's over between Michael and me," she blurted.

"Have you two talked about things?"

"Sort of." She frowned, watching as Michael played a card with a flourish.

"Who ended it?"

"It's mutual. Are you surprised?"

He shrugged. "I sort of guessed. We all saw it coming. Are you sorry?"

She glanced at the others, flipping cards, and shook her head. "It's time for both of us to move on." She pressed the tea to her cheek. "Sounds so crazy, like something out of *The O.C.* or *Buffy*. To be, like, dating in this world when people are plotting viruses and trying to overthrow the government."

"Whoa, you *have* grown up," Diego said, a little miffed. "You start off as this incredibly gorgeous and sexy girl who needs someone and morph into this cranky, doomsday philosopher of pop culture."

"And that's a bad thing or a good one?"

He laughed. "Good, I think."

Liza sighed, glad that she'd come to terms with Diego. She'd been developing a small crush on him during their journey, probably an escape from Michael's meltdown, but she didn't want things to be strained between them. "What do you think would have happened on *The O.C.* if they'd had a chance to finish their season?"

"You're talking to a guy who doesn't even know what *O.C.* stands for. But since my nonnie used to watch some of those shows, I can tell you that someone would have broken up. And someone would have slept with someone else and then gotten discovered by their ex. And of course, there's the addictive behavior and the car crashes."

Liza sighed again as she leaned toward the window. "Those were the good old days."

SIXTEEN

THE SPACE BETWEEN THE CARS WAS COLD; OCCASIONALLY SNOW would drift down from somewhere. The wheels and the ground were only a few frightening feet away, and it was extremely loud, exposed to the elements—one of the few places unlikely to be bugged. Michael had a cigarette all ready to light while they talked so that if soldiers came through, he had an excuse to be out there. The others would come soon—Diego and Irene as a couple, then Keely and her mom from the other direction, then Liza.

He'd been thinking about her, thinking of the courage she had to summon to return to the dysfunctional family nightmare she'd narrowly escaped. He had to give her credit; she was stronger than any of them had suspected.

Irene and Diego appeared just then, hand in hand like a couple on vacation. *You'd never guess they were about to go take down a homicidal madman.*

"Hey, we were just going to the café car," Irene said loudly, over the rumble of the wheels.

"See you back inside," Michael said, nodding.

As they squeezed past, he whispered: "We should arrive in St. Louis by tomorrow at three-fifteen. It's mainly an official stop, so radio silence on all things NM until we cross the river to the west. Just follow me or Dr. Gilmore."

"Any plan on how we're going to get back in?" Diego whispered back, punching him lightly in the stomach and giving him a low-five as Irene opened the other door.

"Not a clue. Open to ideas. Keep thinking." As much as Michael hated to admit it, Diego had proved his ability to strategize on the long trek by the way he'd thwarted their pursuers from Novo Mundum. And Michael never wasted resources.

The sky above was dark blue streaked with a few clouds still faintly white from a sun that had faded hours ago. Michael shivered. Before the Big Empty he had never been in a place where it had been so dark—the power never went out for very long in New York City even after Strain 7. On a deserted beach in the Hamptons you could still see the great glow of the city, projecting an orange nimbus across the heavens.

"It's completely *Wuthering Heights* out here," Keely shouted, stepping through the door that Irene and

Diego had exited through just a few minutes ago. "Very exhilarating!"

"I thought L.A. girls hated weather!" Michael shouted back, wrapping his arms around himself against the cold. Where was her mom? She was supposed to come with her mom. Why didn't anyone ever just follow his plans without changing anything or questioning anything?

"Gothic England's a nice place to visit, but I wouldn't want to live there." Keely shrugged, wrapping her own arms around her chest. But she was smiling, the wind whipping tendrils of hair around her face—very much like someone on the moors. "Well, maybe if I had a horse, and a mansion, and a studly guy in breeches and morning coat with a mad black stallion . . ."

"Would you settle for a guy in a borrowed sweater on a crappy train?"

Wait, what had made him say that?

"Depends. Is he haunted by the mad ghost of a long lost love?"

"No. Just the red-haired princess of a social experiment gone horribly wrong."

"Good enough," Keely said, laughing. "You know, I hate to say it, but she's changed a *lot* recently. . . ."

"Yeah, I know." Enough relationship talk already. There had been so much in his head—going around and around, making him feel bad about how he had treated Liza, how he had let the group down, how the couple of the year almost wasn't . . . "Come on, Keely. If we weren't in the situation we're in, there's no way you two would be friends. There's no reason to start acting like *everybody's* big sister. At least not around me."

"You big cynic," Keely said, crinkling her nose. "So, uh, speaking of girlfriends . . ."

What? *What?* They were all alone out here, in this amazing, electrically charged environment. . . .

". . . do you always date nut jobs?"

"You're a pain in the ass, Gilmore." Michael was sort of relieved—and sort of disappointed.

"Someone has to keep you honest, Bishop." She leaned forward and her lips tickled his ear. "So what's the plan, number one?"

Keely's arms were wrapped around the wide stripe of the rugby shirt that she had found in the apartment, several sizes too big. Her hands were tucked far into the long sleeves, like a college girl.

"When we get off the train tomorrow, follow me or your mom. No talking about anything NM until we cross the river ten miles to the west."

"Your bandage totally doesn't match your outfit," she whispered back, indicating the new sort-of-flesh-tone thing that covered his cheek. "Do something about that, would you? It makes us all look bad."

And with that parting shot she was out the other door. Probably to tell her mom. A wave of depression unexpectedly came over Michael; that was the way they'd all been when Gabe was part of the team. Jokes and sexual tension. *He should really be here,* he thought sadly.

Here at last came Liza, right on schedule, two cups

of hot tea in her hand. "You want a tea?" she asked, holding up one of the cups. "I figured you might be chilly out here."

"Great. Thanks." He took it from her, just to wrap his hands around the warm cardboard. Steam drifted up from the lid, blurring his vision of her for a moment.

"I think we need to be square with each other," she said. "I mean, with the future so murky, I think we should set our relationship straight."

Michael blew off the steam, relieved that she had brought it up. "Yeah, I guess we should admit that it's over." He'd known it for a while; realized it before they'd veered off the subject yesterday in her bedroom. "But I've got to tell you, Liza. . . ." He paused, not sure how to put it.

"Don't tell me you've concocted some patronizing 'good luck next time' speech."

He bit his lower lip. Why couldn't he just come out and say he was sorry for the pile of crazy he had been? For yelling at her, for being mean for no reason and not even being "there" when she needed him most? "The truth is, we don't belong together. But with all that said, I want you to know I'm sorry for . . . making you leave your dad."

"Don't get all patronizing. That's not your fault, Michael, and you know it." She frowned. "Regardless of what happens, I'm glad I left—I had to do it. Don't ever think otherwise. Besides, I've had a zillion experiences out here with you guys . . . not all good ones, but ones that made me grow."

He nodded. "You *have* changed, Liza. You've really learned to stand on your own two feet."

"You've gone through a few incarnations too. From entrepreneur to border guard to superman . . ."

"Until I fell from grace," he said. "I turned out to be human, right?" Michael asked with a faint smile.

"Complex and flawed," she said. "And my life is way too complex right now." She stared out at the landscape that raced past them, the rise of dark hills, the sloping valleys of snow, glowing blue in the night.

Yes, he could understand that Liza had a lot on her mind these days. "So we're square. And I have to give you bonus points. Not bad for your first breakup," he said with a faint smile.

"Again with the patronizing!" She stamped her foot. "And here I was, about to give you the best news of the day."

He nodded, a skeptical grin. "Uh-huh. And that would be . . ."

Liza leaned forward to whisper into his ear. "I have an idea about how to get us back into Novo Mundum."

SEVENTEEN

IT WAS STRANGE GETTING OFF AT THE ST. LOUIS STOP *OFFICIALLY*, like actual people with travel papers and someplace to go. They were surrounded by soldiers of all different ranks and divisions but alike in their green, gray, and khaki uniforms. The six of them stood out badly—as badly as the hunting party, who protested loudly and obnoxiously when they were stopped and questioned. Keely could never imagine acting that way to an intelligence officer. Even her mom, with official papers for all of them, was polite and patient as the Gestapo-esque man-and-woman team spent an hour drilling them with questions and another going through their bags.

When they were finally released, the train station was deserted again, soldiers trucked off to their base, the place as empty and decrepit as only a train station outside the Big Empty would be.

The six of them moved off down the road for several miles, as if to the local government HQ.

"Couldn't we requisition a jeep or something?" Michael asked.

"Don't push your luck, Bishop," her mom snapped, but Keely could see the very slight twinkle in her eye. Mom liked Michael, in a puppy-dog-you-need-to-train kind of way. Keely knew exactly how she felt. . . . "At some point someone's going to trace where I went and what I asked for. The train tickets and papers for all of you was pushing it. Let's not wave a big yellow flag."

Keely watched as Michael digested what her mom had just said and suddenly considered the consequences. "What's going to happen when you get back?"

"House arrest, maybe? I don't know." She shrugged, looking exhausted. "They can't do too much to me—they need me too much."

"And you were willing to risk that—just like that—because of what happened with Twin Elms Two? But not because of what we told you beforehand?" Michael pushed.

Dr. Gilmore cocked her head, studying Michael. "Please don't tell me you're so jaded at . . . nineteen, or whatever you are, that the death of several hundred people doesn't mean anything to you anymore." Keely could have cheered; her mom had the haunted, haggard look of someone who had dealt with far more deaths, but there was an anger beneath it that still lived. How could she have missed it when they lived together?

Michael opened his mouth to argue further, his ego suddenly bridled by the older woman's words, but Liza shook her head and closed her eyes—don't. Keely laughed aloud.

This trip was so different from their recent one. They were all dressed more appropriately, for one thing, having raided Irene's aunt's house for anything that was even slightly warm and boot-like. The snow wasn't deep in the paths they took; here and there the ground was even bare. The sun was shining and the temperature was in the high forties—still miserable by L.A. standards—but by the time they had walked out of the station and down the road back toward Clearwater, she was already warm with the exercise.

"This reminds me of the trip to Novo Mundum the first time," Irene said beside her. She was holding hands with Diego, who was still fairly quiet but smiled more and seemed to have locked the madness away; his eyes were clear. Not that his alphabet ever really had all of its vowels—but this at least was an improvement.

"I was just thinking that." Keely sighed. "Something about the day—and the weather, and the fact that we know where we're going. We have a direction, an end point, and a purpose."

"I like your mom," Diego said, out of nowhere. "She's pretty cool. And she has no illusions about what we need to do and what our chances are."

"Uh, yeah." Keely ran her hand through her hair,

loosening it from the hat she wore. "Thanks, I guess. Especially that part about the whole going-in-to-die thing."

"I'm sure Michael has some sort of brilliant plan," Diego said with a sarcastic smile. Keely found it a lot easier to deal with than the weird, repressed competition that had been brewing between the two guys.

"Hey, less talking, more walking," Michael called, turning back to look at them. "Remember? Radio silence . . . ?"

Keely, Irene, and Diego cracked up. It was *so* Michael.

That night there was a high moon overhead waxing *gibbous*—another SAT word Keely would never need to worry about again. Everything was so bright that Diego allowed a fire—it wouldn't have shown up at all against the white-and-blue nightscape. They had one tent, a Boy Scout "starter," scavenged from the back of a closet. Keely and her mom were forced to take it: Liza had this new independent-person thing to prove, Michael and Diego wouldn't have taken a place from the girls if their lives depended on it, and Irene was going to sleep snuggled up close to Diego anyway.

He went out to hunt for game. Michael helped set up the tent, Irene started the fire, and Keely cooked dinner—a sort of a pan stew from the various supplies they had. Keely's mom watched the stars, stirring the fire when asked and acting generally upbeat, as if she was someone who'd been forced to go on a camping trip and decided to make the best of it. It was like the further from civilization they went, the more back to her old self—her old *mom* self—Dr. Gilmore became. Weird.

"What's the deal?" Keely asked, sitting next to her with a plate of food when they were all done cooking. Diego returned with a pair of rabbits, which they cooked for later use.

"What?" her mom said defensively.

"You seem, I don't know . . ." Keely searched for words carefully. She didn't want to upset their delicate new post-reunion relationship over something dumb. "*Relaxed.* As Diego pointed out, we have no idea what's going to happen or what we're going to face. It's just the six of us with no clue against a crazy man with a deadly virus."

Her mom shrugged. "It's the first vacation I've had in years."

"*Mom,*" Keely said, shocked.

"Look at this." She indicated the woods around them. "I haven't gone hiking or anything in a *decade.* No cars, no people—no one staring down over my shoulder every minute of the day, tapping my phone lines—"

"Told you," Michael said to Keely, climbing into the circle with his own plate of food.

"—wondering who is reporting on you to the government, having your house *searched* periodically . . ."

"Did that happen when I lived there?" Keely asked, eyes widening. Her mother didn't answer, choosing instead just to regard her steadily over the top of her mug.

There were times—Keely had assumed it was her *mom*—she had come home from school to find things subtly changed about her room, notebooks flipped through. . . .

Why couldn't her mom have given her some hint of what was going on? Of how awful things were for her at work, what was really going on with her and the government . . . Okay, maybe she hadn't wanted to get Keely involved, knowing things she wasn't supposed to know—but she could have found a way to tell her *something*. Didn't her mom see how Keely could have been trusted with a secret?

"What's it like out there, anyway?" Irene asked, chewing on a piece of particularly crunchy stewed tofu bar. "Houston was a pit. From what Keely says, L.A. was slightly better off."

"Yeah." Liza scrootched forward. "You guys still get TV and stuff, right? I haven't seen a show in *years*. . . ."

Keely's mom laughed. "Okay, maybe there are a few good things that remain in the 'civilized' world. They just reopened the Ivy, in Hollywood."

"That place where all the stars eat out—uh, used to eat out?" Michael asked excitedly despite himself. Keely smiled. So there *was* a normal little boy somewhere underneath all his posturing and need to lead. Some of that had shown last night in the train. In another time, in another place—and without Liza—it might have been incredibly romantic. He had actually let his guard down for two seconds—which, despite what people said about Diego, was actually far rarer for Michael than the country boy.

"Yeah. You thought Matsuhisa used to have a long reservation list; you should see this." Keely's mom turned to her, rolling her eyes. "Months. The Stinking Rose on La Cienega reopened too—and Mezzaluna on Melrose."

"Wow, those are just like names from the movies," Liza said dreamily. "I can't believe you *lived* there, Keely."

"Oh, it was a blast," Keely muttered. But for just a moment her mother brought back blue afternoons, glittering palm trees, red sunsets over the ocean, and cruising down the PCH in her dad's Cabrio with the top down. Ultra-skinny teens wearing barely there string clothes—going to restaurants and malls. *French fries,* even. Doubled doubles at In-N-Out Burger.

"And they've started shooting *The Young and the Restless* again," her mom said, thinking. "They're going to actually address what happened the last few years, writing Strain 7 into the storyline. A surprising number of cast members survived, and after a few months of political volleyball, the government finally decided to allow them to broadcast on channel 28 to improve morale. That's UHF, by the way, for you satellite-age kids. Anyway, it does lift the spirits. We keep the show on in the lab."

"Oh my God, that was my favorite soap," Irene said, like Michael, before she could stop herself. Everyone stared at her. "What?" she asked indignantly. "There's nothing that says a med school geek can't like a little daytime drama."

"Jack's still alive, you'll be glad to know," Keely's mom said with a smile.

"No *way . . . !*"

Although she—and Diego, and Michael—had no real interest in soap operas before Strain 7, Keely found herself hanging on her mom's every word, every boring plot twist and worn-out romantic angle. Novo Mundum stressed the arts—but not so much the normal, entertaining, narrative fiction.

Lazy and slow embers separated themselves from the top of the fire's flames and drifted skyward with her mom's words, joining the stars above them before disappearing into the night. So there were a few stars left in Hollywood. . . . Maybe there was some hope for this world after all.

EIGHTEEN

LIZA COULDN'T BELIEVE HOW EASY THE RIVER CROSSING WAS this time—without pursuers forcing every quick, unplanned-for step, they could choose the right place. Diego found an oxbow where the water narrowed at one pinch and was frozen solid for several inches. It felt as secure as walking across the marble floor at a bank.

They broke for lunch soon after that, in a strange, festive mood. Diego estimated that they were less than two days from Novo Mundum. That close to some sort of showdown, and no one seemed too badly bothered yet.

Liza wondered how much longer that was going to last and when tensions would begin to burst within the group again.

There had been another slight reshuffle among the six, a natural evolution that Liza suspected might have had something to do with the fact that she and Michael had broken it off. Keely and her mom still stuck together, but Irene had joined them, showering Dr. Gilmore with all sorts of medical questions she had been apparently saving up. *Somebody get that girl to med school,* Liza thought, though according to Irene, all the med schools had disbanded with Strain 7. Another nonsensical thing to Liza, who figured they needed *more* doctors to research and help people, not less.

Anyway, with Irene playing to the doc, Michael began to walk with Diego, trying to learn from *him:* how to read the weather, how to tell what direction they were going without a compass, which prints meant what kind of animal. Just what he should have been doing on the way out, except that he'd curled into himself in a ball of depression.

And strangely, Liza and Keely occasionally fell into step now. Most of the time it was silent—they didn't really have much to talk about. But it wasn't an uncomfortable silence, the way it would have been two weeks ago. Liza felt Keely's newfound respect, and although she wasn't quite sure what she'd done to earn it, she was okay with moving through time, down the road, headed to the same place together. A separate peace.

Sometimes they did talk, though; Liza had never realized what a different and interesting world it was outside Greenwich College or Novo Mundum. Before Strain 7 she'd had it drilled into her that everyone who wasn't in academics—specifically, the sciences—wasn't really worth talking to. After the plague and visions of the horrors that lay in the rest of the country, she and everyone at Novo Mundum—unsurprisingly—had no desire to deal with the outside world again.

But listening to Dr. Gilmore that first night brought back memories of wanting to go to Disneyland, of wondering, like any teenager, if the world of moviemaking was as glamorous and magical as it seemed. Of wanting to swim in an ocean.

Keely was surprised when Liza continued to question her about life in L.A. as a kid and teenager . . . and Liza was pleased at Keely's slow opening up. She even talked about her sister, Bree, a little, and when her eyes got glassy, Liza didn't press her.

"Okay, Bishop, what's the plan?" Diego asked, tossing a snowball at Michael's head as they settled down into "the Circle," as Irene had begun calling it. They moved so smoothly and with such synchronization—why had it taken so long? *Do we really need a grown-up along to make us behave?* Liza wondered, a little bitterly.

"Not me," Michael said, dodging. He pointed at Liza. "She's got an idea this time."

Everyone stared at her and she froze.

"Uh." Liza cleared her throat. "Um . . ."

"Let's hear it," Dr. Gilmore said kindly.

She hadn't thought it was going to be like this. When the nuggets of the idea had begun to form in her brain, irritating and rolling around like particles of sand before becoming pearls, Liza had been so cautiously thrilled with herself that she hadn't actually planned ahead to the part where she told everyone. In her head she told Michael in private, and he praised her or something. Not this.

"All I meant was—I should go back in. By myself," she said, trying not to stammer. "Like Maggie did." She forced herself to ignore the wince of pain on Michael's face and continue. "I'll tell them that you guys kidnapped me as kind of insurance against being captured or shot."

"How did you . . . escape us?" Diego asked slowly, tracing something in the snow with a stick. He might not have said anything to anyone—but it was obvious he was ashamed of his own role with Maggie.

Liza had no intention of letting anyone break her jaw.

"When you guys got far enough away, you just let me go since you had no further use for me. You invited me to come with you, but I just wanted to go back home to Daddy."

Michael was nodding slowly in approval. At one time that would have thrilled her, but she found herself looking at Dr. Gilmore for confirmation.

"What are you going to do when you're there?" Keely's mom asked, shifting in her seat. Once again her hands were wrapped around a tin mug of something hot and watery—like a security blanket. Liza got a sudden flash of her standing in a room of infected patients and test tubes, clasping a ceramic mug like that, wondering how she was going to get through the day.

"First of all, figure out how to get you guys back in. Like turning off the electric fence or something. And while I'm there, do some snooping around—try to figure out what my dad's plans are next, see if I can get vaccinated against this Strain 8—see if I can get extras for you guys . . ."

"Dr. MacTavish will do it if you talk to her," Michael said.

Irene shook her head. "She won't trust you at first. . . . You need to let her know somehow that it's okay, that we're all part of this." She frowned, thinking. "Tell her—tell her that your teeth are itchy."

Everyone stared at Irene this time. It was kind of a relief.

"It's a common question you ask hypochondriacs," Irene said, a little defensively. "Amber and I were joking about it one day. Sort of black humor about Strain 7. Asking corpses if their teeth itched."

"This is a side of you I've never seen before," Diego said, intrigued.

"The best thing you could do there is get us a lab notebook or something," Dr. Gilmore said, pushing her dark auburn hair out of her face, behind her ear, in a gesture that was so reminiscent of Keely that for just a moment they might have been sisters. "Keely told me that's how you figured out what was going on. If Slattery's notes are detailed, they can at least give me some idea of what we're facing in there. Any foreknowledge would be an advantage at this point."

"Even if we know about what the virus is or whatever, how would that help us stop it?" Diego demanded.

Dr. Gilmore shrugged. "We could set the whole lab on fire. If that's the only place it was kept, it would probably destroy it."

"If he's a clever lunatic, he'll keep a vial somewhere else," Michael said, frowning with thought. Liza also frowned, but for different reasons. She really wished they would stop calling her father names like that. He was still her dad. "That's what the super-villains always do."

"You're planning this all based on *comic books*?" Keely asked with a smile.

Michael shook his head and pointed at Liza. "*She's* planning it. I'm just the uppity sidekick."

"Children," Dr. Gilmore said, clearing her throat.

"You should also see what the military situation is," Michael said, serious again. "If there are extra guards, what their shifts are, if things are hyper-tight there now . . ."

"And how is she supposed to give us all this information?" Dr. Gilmore asked. "Slattery's not going to let her go anywhere *near* the outside perimeter again. Even if she fools him—and especially if she doesn't."

"We have these." Michael pulled out the Incredible Hulk walkie-talkies they had found in the apartment next door. "They're good for half a mile if it's relatively flat."

"You have *got* to be kidding me," Dr. Gilmore said, taking one and turning it over in her hands. It was pretty ridiculous looking—bright neon green and yellow.

"What happened to radio silence?" Irene asked.

"We'll come up with a really shorthand code," Keely said, and Michael nodded. It was obvious that they had already discussed this. "If it's a quick burst, they'll mistake it for some sort of glitch."

"The reason we caught those MacCauley soldiers last time was because they *continued to talk* on our channel," Michael explained.

"You feel up to this?" Irene asked gently.

"Completely!" Liza said, indignant. "I think," she added honestly, a second later.

NINETEEN

They pitched camp in early afternoon two miles from Novo Mundum so Liza could approach it under the cover of darkness the next morning. No fire was allowed this time; it was too close. No one argued with Diego over these decisions anymore, Irene noticed—but whether that was because Michael now politely deferred to him in all things outdoors or because everyone was afraid of the insane anger that they had seen, she wasn't sure.

Keely's mom was cool, at least. She was everything Irene always wanted to be professionally.

"You should come back with us when this is all over," the older woman said, unfurling her bedroll. "I'm completely short-handed. There's no system in place to train the next generation of researchers and doctors at this point—I know it's not the field you're interested in, but believe me, it's definitely a career with a future."

Irene couldn't think of anything to say. Especially after events at Novo Mundum, she wanted to deal with patients, not laboratories. But what an opportunity! And Dr. Gilmore really sounded serious. That would be so strange, going back to L.A. with her and Keely. Of course, she'd be working for the government, but there would be a chance to learn and work with other real doctors. . . .

In a daze, Irene dragged her own bedroll over to where Diego had set up his.

"Isn't it gorgeous?" He sighed. Diego was stretched out on the ground, hands behind his head. It *was* a beautiful day—the sky was an incredible dark gray-blue Irene had never seen before, and the afternoon sunlight warmed everything it touched, causing the icicle-laden trees it lit to slowly drip, melt, and sparkle. A single breath tasted good: of clear, clean, wet wilderness, bringing up distant memories of skiing as a child.

"It is," Irene agreed, wrenching herself out of the excitement of what Keely's mom had just offered her. Diego looked so happy—his cheeks were flushed rosy and his eyes were bright. A single tiny drop of ice hung off one of his long eyelashes, but he blinked it away before it could melt.

"I could stay out here forever," Diego murmured. His smile turned a little sad when he saw how she was trying to keep her face blank and her eyes neutral. "I know that's probably not what you want. . . . But maybe you could be a doctor in one of the border towns or something? I'll bet there's a lot of places where, you know, we could live at least a little bit in the country. . . ."

Irene tried to smile back as she got into her bedroll next to him. *Great. This is going to be a fun discussion when we finally have it.* On the flip side, there was a good chance they wouldn't come out of this alive, so he couldn't bring it up again and she wouldn't have to make the decision.

As if Diego could read her thoughts, he reached over and took her hand and cupped it in his own, kissing it. "We'll get out of this okay. I *promise.*"

Liza slithered into her own sleeping bag—but close to Michael. His own was a very sexy SpongeBob SquarePants number with a built-in, inflatable pillow. There was barely enough room for a grown boy like him.

"I really am proud of you," Michael whispered.

"Thanks," she said eagerly. Then her face drooped. "But what choice did we have, really?"

"We could have . . ." He thought hard, trying to come up with something quick. But he'd had the whole train ride to think and hadn't been able to come up with anything more solid than "sneak in somehow" and overpower the biggest guards, or somehow take either Slattery hostage, or try to blow up the lab as Dr. Gilmore had suggested. If the electric fence was on, getting in would be *extremely* tricky, involving climbing trees and dropping down from branches, somehow all unseen. They were like the government invading the Branch Davidians—without any weapons. Or backup. Or—anything, really. "We could have done *something*," he insisted.

"I wonder if it's worth it," Liza said pensively. "I know my dad's insane . . . but if you took him and Uncle Frank away, would Novo Mundum be so bad?"

"By itself, no," Michael said, thinking about it. He turned over onto his back. "It's not a bad little social experiment at all. I mean, given a chance, I'd rather not spend the rest of my life in a dinky commune growing my own wheatgrass and being terrified of the government—but since I'm a wanted man, there isn't really a whole lot else."

"You guys have shown me the rest of the world. It kind of sucks."

"Hey, now, you've just seen Houston," Michael said, not liking where the conversation was going. "There are a lot of people in New York—and L.A., I guess—normal, good people, who aren't happy with what's going on. You should come to New York sometime," he said, forgetting for a moment that he didn't live there anymore—that he could never go back. "They're talking about maybe opening up the Empire State Building on weekends again, as soon as there's enough power. I'll bet if there aren't too many fires, you can still get a pretty good view of Manhattan. . . ."

"Michael." Liza fixed him with a look that he hadn't seen from a girl since his mother died. "Get serious for a moment. Is *any*one in any position to throw off the government?"

"No," Michael said, reluctantly pulling himself out of the daydream. "I'm just saying you shouldn't write off the rest of the world—the way your dad is," he added carefully.

Liza took that with a nasty look, though she seemed to consider it. "None of us have a place in this new world," she finally said. "Irene wants to be a doctor and just basically broke up with her family. You're running from the law. Keely doesn't want to be with her mom, and her mom doesn't want to work for the government but feels she has to."

"And Diego wants to be Mr. Nature but can't seem to let go of us, really," Michael added. He hadn't missed the interplay between Liza and Diego—and while he was better friends with Diego now, he couldn't resist the dig. "*Irene,* actually."

"And I can't go home again. But I *am* going home again. To let the Trojan horse in." Liza sighed, lying back and throwing an arm over her eyes.

Michael let out a deep sigh. "You're being incredibly brave, you know."

"Thanks," she said. "I don't know if I feel like it, but . . ."

"Well, you are."

Michael couldn't help thinking of the irony. Just as the two of them realized things weren't really right between them, Liza suddenly started demonstrating how she completely *wasn't* like Maggie, that she was capable of learning and growing beyond herself.

Maybe that was who she'd really been all along, though, and she'd just needed a chance to prove it. Maybe Michael *hadn't* just fallen for another Maggie.

In other words, even if it was over between them, maybe Liza wasn't the only person who'd done some important growing.

"There seem to be a lot of getting-busy goings-on," Keely's mom remarked as the two of them hunkered down in the strange, end-of-the-world white afternoon light.

"Mom," Keely warned.

"I'm just saying. You could cut the hormones out here with a chain saw."

Keely muttered to herself and turned to face away from her mother, who had that bird-bright, interested look on her face that at one time had helped her daughters get A's on their science projects . . . and later on had embarrassed Keely in front of her friends and boyfriend.

"Did you . . . become close . . . to anyone at 'Novo Mundum'?"

Keely closed her eyes in annoyance. *"Mom!"*

"I'm just asking. Must have been nice, being with all of those young people . . . Eric's death hit you pretty hard. . . ."

"Did you hook up with anyone in your lab?" Keely shot back.

"No—but that's different." Keely could hear her mother's voice soften. "You're sixteen. I'm forty-seven. I had known your father for twenty years. It's a little harder to get over."

So the future of the human race rests with teenagers and those who aren't deep in mourning, Keely thought sarcastically. But her mom was kind of right. *Everyone* had lost someone to Strain 7—Keely wasn't different or special because she'd lost her boyfriend. A lot of other people her age had managed to move on—why hadn't she?

"There was this guy, Gabe," she murmured, mostly into her pillow. "We sort of almost hooked up."

"I'll keep the dialogue going by not asking the parental 'what exactly do you mean by hooked up?'" her mom said. Keely could hear her rustling under the blankets, sitting up on one elbow. Sometimes at night when Keely was younger, her mom would come in—knowing full well she was still awake—and prop herself up on the bed like that, like they were at a sleepover, trying to connect with her. "What happened?"

Keely took a deep breath—only one tear fell. "He died. Slattery's brother turned on an electric fence specifically to kill him and Michael." Her mother couldn't hide the sharp intake of breath—Keely screwed her eyes shut and refused to be pitied. "We weren't that close." *Yet.*

Her mom was quiet for a moment, taking it all in.

"I'm sorry," she finally said. She took a deep breath—then let it out, as if she'd decided to say something else. "I wish you'd had more time before life got complicated for you. You were supposed to have four years of college for life to slowly sneak up on you. Seven killed half the population of the world—and forced the remaining half to grow up far quicker than they should have."

"You're not going to go off on some sort of 'loss of innocence' rant, are you?" Keely asked with a faint smile. "While I appreciate our mother-daughter bonding time, I could also use some serious shut-eye."

"Who, me? Never. Look at how done I am. Sleepy time." Her mom grinned and blew a kiss at her. "G'night, Keely. Sweet dreams. Don't let the—uh, never mind."

"Good night." Keely smiled and lay back down again. It was crazy, but somehow having her mom along really did make everything all right. She wiggled around a little bit to get comfortable, hiding her eyes in the old dog-smelling blanket to block out the light. Sleep came easy these days.

"That Michael is kind of a cutie," her mom suddenly said. "Reminds me of your dad when he was younger."

Keely groaned and covered her face and ears with the blanket too.

TWENTY

MICHAEL WAS AWAKE BEFORE DIEGO ACTUALLY CAME OVER TO rouse them. Something inside made his eyes snap open and journey from sleep to consciousness instantly. At first he thought there had been a noise or something—but there was nothing. The silence was complete except for an occasional whisper in the tops of the pines caused by a chill early morning breeze.

The stars were fantastic—numbering in the thousands, pinprick sharp and bright enough to cast beams and soft shadows on the ground, a harlequin pattern of tissue paper over the snow. It was deadly cold but somehow less frightening than when he'd gotten frostbite. Like the sky had been opened. He wiggled his toes in the three layers of socks he now wore—Irene and Dr.

Gilmore had both warned him about how easy it would be for him to get frostbite in the same spot again.

Diego's outline obscured the sky, rising above him.

"I'm awake," Michael whispered. "God, it's beautiful out. Unbelievable."

The other boy grinned. "You're *finally* getting it, city boy! I'll go wake the others."

Michael sighed and turned to Liza, who was breathing softly, still sound asleep. Like a child, she could sleep soundly anywhere as long as there were people around her. He tapped her shoulder. "Come on, Liza, it's time."

They all moved slowly, hunched over with arms wrapped around their middles, quiet yetis starting their day. From somewhere—maybe the trees—a thin veil of light snow swirled around them, making Diego happy. It might not completely obscure their tracks, but if their luck held, they could be mistaken for a herd of something else bedding down for the night.

Sleepy and caught in the strange spell of the silent, star-filled night, they walked without speaking, accompanying Liza for all but the last half mile. When they finally approached the blown-up road that led down the peninsula to the old campus of Greenwich College and the site of Novo Mundum, all but Keely's mom looked at each other and paused for a moment, each feeling something big and different wash over him or her.

"What's the holdup?" Dr. Gilmore whispered.

"This was going to be paradise," Irene whispered. "A safe haven for me and my dad and brother."

"I was going to escape L.A. and the government and start a whole new world," Keely added.

"It was home," Liza said simply, shrugging.

"This is where we leave you, kiddo," Michael said, trying to force emotion back down, not to scare or frighten her. "When you go up the road, make as obvious a path as possible."

She nodded and adjusted her pack. Michael looked at it with a critical eye—did it seem too light? He had taken out the things that they would need more than she but left enough stuff to make it believable that she had come all this way by herself—including the compass, which made Diego uneasy. "They would *never* believe Liza had done this otherwise—and it's still a big thing to swallow," Keely had pointed out, out of Liza's hearing.

"Good luck," she said now, giving her a hug. "This is incredibly brave of you."

Michael expected Liza to say something like "Don't patronize me" or "I can do it!" or something equally Liza-esque, but she just nodded with big shining eyes and set her jaw like a soldier.

Irene hugged her too and so did Diego—she didn't let go so quickly from him, but Michael found himself more amused than annoyed. Dr. Gilmore shook her hand and wished her luck.

"Oh, I almost forgot." Michael took a deep breath, terrified that he had almost not remembered it. He pulled the gun out of his waistband and handed it to her. "Keep this close to you, somewhere where your dad and uncle won't feel it if they hug you or something."

Liza's eyes got wider. "I'm—I'm just doing recon," she stammered—but took it, slowly and carefully.

"Don't forget, our main goal is to stop Dr. Slattery," Dr. Gilmore said gently. "If you see an opportunity to blow up his experiments or whatever—*take* it."

Liza nodded and slipped the gun into an ankle pocket on her cargo pants. Michael was sure he was the only one who heard her murmur, "I can't shoot anyone. . . ."

TWENTY-ONE

IT WAS CRAZY, LIZA KNEW, BUT FIFTEEN MINUTES AWAY FROM where everyone said goodbye, she felt colder. Trudging down the road was hard—even with the occasional jeep tire tracks to walk in. Everything was too quiet, and between the silence and the difficulty of pushing through the snow it seemed to take forever to reach the gate. She felt like she had died and this was some sort of perpetual, punishing afterlife. One of her few memories with her mother in it involved being tiny and trying to toddle through the snow. Her parents stood at the end of the driveway and beckoned for her to come, shouting and smiling and encouraging her—but Liza panicked. The snow was too deep and she began to run, falling, tripping, swimming in the giant drifts.

Liza wrapped her arms around herself more tightly and picked up the pace, lifting her feet very carefully so she wouldn't repeat the childhood mistake. Unlike then, there was *no one* around her now. Having run away from her father and broken up with Michael, she felt stripped and raw: these last twenty steps were the most lonely ones she had ever taken, the most alone she had ever been.

She quieted her fears by imagining the best-possible scenes of her triumph: throwing open the gates for her friends, sending out people to get them, everything being okay, and the whole group of them—Keely, Diego, Irene, Dr. Gilmore, and Michael—cheering their savior.

The sky had just begun to lighten by the time she drew up to the main gate: like something out of a fairy tale or Narnia, a chain-link fence covered in barbed wire rose out of the ground, the only man-made thing visible in the otherwise pure woods. Even the road was covered completely by snow.

Somewhere a few feet in front of it was an invisible, deadly trip wire that would electrocute her in an instant if she came any closer.

Shouldn't the snow melt off it . . . ? she wondered, trying to think logically like Diego or Keely. But honestly, she had no idea.

On to plan two.

She took a deep breath, opened her mouth wide, and began screaming.

TWENTY-TWO

DIEGO FROWNED, LOOKING AT THE BARE PATCHES OF GROUND that leapt like a rabbit from tree to tree, huddling in close, as if for protection. *If someone wanted to and took the time, he could travel the length of the forest without leaving tracks in the snow.* All the way from the train station, for instance.

He knelt on the ground and flipped over a dried leaf that floated above the sea of pine needles like an old shrunken boat. The edge of it had been cracked off—it had been *stepped on* by something. Or someone.

Diego had gone back along their path several miles, brushing snow over their tracks with a branch. He had been more afraid of scouts coming back from missions *to* Novo Mundum, but if this was a person following them and not a random animal, he or she was far more stealthy and clever than the jackbooted idiots who guarded the community. Even Tabori, cleverest of the bunch, couldn't have done it.

He looked up: there was a bare patch high up on the closest tree, almost like it had been shaken loose when someone leaned against the trunk.

Diego sighed deeply. There was no point in warning *everyone* about it, but he would tell Michael. "Keep him in the loop" as the city boy was always saying

He liked scouting, the hours alone in the woods, the silence. He smiled to himself, thinking of Liza and how she'd begged to come along. Maybe she'd actually learned something on their little excursions together—it hadn't escaped his notice that when she'd walked away from them, it was with one foot in front of the other, silently.

Diego murmured a little prayer for her, pulling out his cross and kissing it, tossing a glance heavenward.

The other four were on snowless ground; Keely and Irene were playing a game of cards that looked suspiciously like go fish and Michael was trying to repair his jacket with a length of dental floss and a needle. Dr. Gilmore sat next to him, watching everyone nervously.

"Hey." He sat on a rock next to Michael.

"Hey." Michael squinched his eyes and carefully fed the needle through one side of his jacket, trying hard not to prick himself on the other. "Get any game?"

"Not this time. Wasn't hunting."

"When you do, could you maybe get a cow next

time? Or a herd of wild, wandering burgers? I'm kind of getting tired of the whole rabbit thing."

Diego started to bridle but realized that the other boy was joking. He *still* couldn't get used to his deadpan delivery or the lengths of sarcasm he used.

"A steak wouldn't suck." Dr. Gilmore sighed.

"Listen." Diego leaned in, making it look like he was observing Michael's handiwork. He might as well let Dr. Gilmore know as well—she could handle it. "Why would anyone from the government follow you—if they were?"

"I'm kind of important. I told you that."

"Yeah, you never explained exactly why," Michael said, exchanging a glance with Diego.

"I told you. . . ."

"Yeah, yeah," Michael said, a little heatedly. "Government keeping all you virologists together in case something else happens. Yet you're important enough to get us train passes—and be tailed. *No one* gets that kind of treatment these days, except for high-up government muckety-mucks and their friends. So what were you really doing?"

Keely and Irene had stopped their game and were looking over worriedly at the raised voices.

"They're afraid someone's been following us," Dr. Gilmore explained.

Diego closed his eyes in frustration and Michael shook his head.

"What, you were going to keep it from them?" she demanded. "I know a lot of stuff has changed out here since Strain 7, but I didn't think we had already regressed to the point of 'not scaring the women'—who are just as strong, capable, and smart as the two of you. Not telling members of your team key information that might keep you all alive is a crazy mistake to make out here."

"I have never treated Keely as anything but an equal," Michael shot back. "Back in Novo Mundum, I chose her to share a mission. One that involved driving hundreds of miles, breaking into a warehouse, and getting shot at."

"It's true, Mom," Keely said in confirmation. Then she frowned. "Although recently the two of you have been doing some weird male-bonding thing, I have to say. . . ."

Diego suddenly felt embarrassed—Dr. Gilmore and Keely were right. Irene had every right to know if her life was in danger—and she was far more levelheaded than Liza. Or Michael, for that matter.

"And as for the people who may or may not be following us," Dr. Gilmore said dryly, "they probably have a lot more going for them than Incredible Hulk walkie-talkies and handguns. Let's just hope your little friend does her job and contacts us soon."

She was right, of course.

But she also didn't answer Michael's question.

TWENTY-THREE

"HEY! DAD! SOMEONE! ANYONE! *HEY!*"

Liza felt a little ridiculous, just shouting whatever came into her head into the darkness of the woods.

"*Hhhheyyyyyyyyyyyy!*"

After about five minutes of this she was rewarded by a sound in the snow: the crunching, half-off steps of men in large boots running. Lights bobbed in the trees ahead like aliens—like any strange shot of *something* running through the woods from a horror movie or TV show.

"Hey," she called again, voice cracking a little. *Wait, why am I here? Didn't we decide my dad was a potential mass murderer? Shouldn't we be as far away from Novo Mundum as possible?* One of her legs began to shake a little, the one she was leaning on. She took a deep breath and held it, not letting the shaking extend to the rest of her body.

"STAY WHERE YOU ARE. DON'T MOVE OR WE'LL SHOOT."

An electronically amplified voice caught her just as one of the lights did: Liza froze, just like the time onstage in fourth grade. She couldn't see anything, blinded by the spot or whatever they were using. Everything was white and bright and hurting her eyes. Don't move or we'll shoot? Couldn't they tell who she was? Didn't they recognize her? *Her?*

"I want to see my daddy," Liza protested.

"HOLD IT RIGHT THERE. DO NOT MOVE."

There was a click and a whistle, mutters over a walkie-talkie.

Liza squeezed her eyes shut, trying to also shut out her vulnerability, her loneliness in the dark, the fact that the next sound could be a gunshot.

All the time since Novo Mundum had been set up, Liza had felt *safe*. The last images they received on the TV a little over a year ago showed horrible things going on outside—angry rioting and looting, piles of corpses in the streets where there wasn't enough infrastructure to get rid of them, strange confrontations with authority as people with guns holed up in big houses, collecting everyone they knew who survived, all wearing surgical masks.

Then the government had re-formed.

MacCauley with a team of nine men seized power,

using the army to institute control from the top down. The damage was man versus government for a very short while: soldiers against people who refused to give up the bodies of their loved ones, against people who refused to move, against people who didn't see the necessity of the rationing, the protein bars, the coupons, the new martial law.

Liza had felt safe against all that here, in the middle of nowhere, protected by the often good-looking men in black boots who reported to her father and loved her uncle Frank and joked with everyone else.

Now, on the other side of their guns, she didn't feel quite so safe.

"It's ME," she shouted desperately. "Liza. Liza Slattery. I'm home—I want to see Dad!" She turned her eyes this way and that, trying to avoid the light without actually moving—afraid for the first time ever that someone was actually going to shoot her. It hadn't been like this even on the trip out—if Ellen or Jonah or anyone had seen her with the rest, they never would have fired at her.

"IS THERE ANYONE WITH YOU?" The voice came again after a moment's hesitation, a murmured discussion punctuated by electronic squawks. She might have misheard, but Liza could have sworn someone said, "It does sound a lot like her, sir."

"No, it's just me. Alone. Please let me in!"

"PUT YOUR HANDS UP AND COME FORWARD."

Liza turned her head finally and did as they said, approaching the gate slowly, one careful footstep at a time. "WE'VE TURNED OFF THE ELECTRICITY. COME FORWARD THROUGH THE GATE."

"You first," Liza shouted back. There was no way she was walking forward over the potentially deadly trip wire. Hopefully they would interpret what she said as a pissy little normal-Liza thing to say. There were some grumbles, but she saw a hand unlock the gate and push it open. It screeched and fell to the side—far more defensive than pretty. Liza raised her hands high and walked in.

"It really is you," one of the guards said, stunned.

"Oh, Mario," Liza said, throwing her arms around him, crying.

Only some of it was for show.

The four soldiers led her back through to the main campus—even though she hadn't been gone all that long, Liza looked around eagerly for changes. She hadn't been away for more than a week or two at a time since her family had first moved to Greenwich College. A blanket of snow covered everything, cleaning and softening the edges. Some of the dark dorms and academic buildings had friendly orange glows in some windows, little sparks of life. Even at this hour there were people going to their shifts or tasks, bundled up and trudging down the carefully shoveled paths, occasionally throwing snowballs at each other.

Liza felt her heart break a little—it was so different from the outside world. Warm and safe and happy.

Two ahead and two behind the soldiers marched her

to the old alumni house. Uncle Frank emerged from the quaint old stained glass door, his face strained with surprise and shock. It looked like he had been called away from paperwork for this, with just his short-sleeved camo top and pants, a hat thrown hastily on at the last minute. He ran forward and picked her up like she was a little girl again, twirling her around and hugging her close to his chest.

"Oh, Liza," he said—was that a *sob* in his voice? "I can't believe you're back!"

She began to cry again. It was strange how much she suddenly realized she missed Uncle Frank. Whatever was true about him, whatever the horrible things he'd planned with her dad, they melted away against his chest and in his strong arms and at his ugly, tear-streaked face. He put her down, leaning over to give her one last squeeze.

"You shouldn't have come back," he whispered into her ear.

Before Liza could react, he had let her go and stood up military straight, facing the lab. The tears dried where they had run; he made no move to wipe them and looked no less manly for it. After a moment her dad came stepping out the front door, clad in an anorak and boots.

He certainly took his time.

"Liza," he said slowly, that winning, cordial grin growing across his lower face. It didn't quite reach his eyes.

"Daddy!" Liza yelled, and ran across the snow to

hug him. It was a lot harder to fake delight at seeing her father. This was forced, and she was afraid her grin was equally plastered on. Liza grabbed him around the middle and turned her head to the side so she wouldn't have to see his face—and so he couldn't pick out the falseness on hers. He put his hands on her shoulders and pressed her to him—it probably looked patriarchal, and solemn, and emotional to everyone watching.

He was good at that.

"I can't say," he announced, his voice choking, "just how it feels to have my daughter back."

TWENTY-FOUR

Amber managed to convince one of the many lovely, cowlike women who were watching her to go get her something that smelled like mint to quell the nausea. After she waddled off, Amber carefully eased herself out of bed and began the slow, shuffling search for Liza. If anyone caught her, she could tell the truth: she really was just overexcited to see her old friend again. *Actually, I'd be more excited if it was* anyone else, Amber thought dryly. If they'd gotten her message and come back, it only made sense that they would send in Liza first, to clear the way and check the situation—but Amber couldn't make heads or tails of all the gossip flying around.

Consensus seemed to indicate that Liza had

escaped from the rest of the group—or that they had let her go after she was no longer useful to them. Some people said that they'd offered for her to come along with them and she'd rejected it, preferring to get back to Novo Mundum or die trying. Others—those who maybe didn't love the NM princess quite as much as her dad—said that they had told her to get lost after escaping Ellen Tabori and her troops.

And unless the silly little girl had changed a *lot* in the last five weeks, Amber was pretty sure she was incapable of making *any* sort of journey alone, through the wilderness or what passed for civilization these days. Besides, there had to be a connection between Liza showing up now and that e-mail Amber had sent to the others—the one that, thanks to the response she'd gotten, had proved they were all alive, giving Amber the kind of relief she'd never experienced in her entire life.

Amber threw a shawl over her shoulders—ridiculous, she looked like an old aunt or something—and tottered down the hallway out into the cold. The change in air temperature made her sneeze; she looked up at the winter light, which she had been exiled from for so long. *Good riddance.* You couldn't tell if it was dawn or dusk: a pale orb, like the egg sacs of the spiders she was always finding in the greenhouses, hung behind the drab gray layer of clouds.

Why couldn't Novo Mundum have been somewhere warm, like Florida or Louisiana? There were vast stretches of land no one went into, and certainly they had just as many anti-government survivalists willing to keep the place a secret.

Little groups huddled here and there, obviously talking about the homecoming—Amber had a feeling that the season had changed, but these groups and their gossip didn't. Her nurses in particular loved to talk about who was sleeping with whom. It might not be exactly free love at Novo Mundum, but it was definitely very cheap.

Just put one foot after the other. Amber aimed for the lab, figuring she had a better chance of finding Liza—or at least getting a truer account of details from the guards there. But it was hard to gauge distances in the strange light, over snow.

As the blood rushed to her face, she saw the ground began to spin, like an ad for vanilla pudding.

"Hey, careful there."

Suddenly Jonah was at her side, supporting her.

"Shit," Amber swore, knowing her little jaunt was over. And not just because she had been found out. What would have happened if she fell?

"What are you doing out of bed?" he asked gently, obviously trying not to antagonize her this one time. She motioned back to the dorm with her chin.

"I just wanted to see Liza, see how she was."

"You and everyone else on campus," Jonah said with a tight grin. She leaned on his arm—not that massive, but hard as a rock and taut against her hand, soft from the flannel he wore.

"This weather sucks," she muttered.

"You don't need to tell a Georgia boy that." He laughed, putting on a thick accent. "No one else came with her," he added, apparently out of nowhere—but it was obviously the subject they were dancing around. Amber kept her face stony.

"They're gone," she said, shrugging. "I just wanted to hear about them—see if they were okay."

"Thought you didn't *care* what happened to 'the roommate who betrayed you,'" Jonah pushed, opening the door for her. Why did he always have to do that? She was trying to avoid saying anything incriminating or nasty. . . . Why couldn't he just have let the whole thing drop?

"And you don't care at all? Not even about what happened to your precious Irene?" Amber spat back. Jonah's eyes darkened.

"I almost had to *shoot* Diego . . . and the others! Don't tell me how to feel about things!"

Amber narrowed her eyes. This was new. And not exactly what had been reported to Frank Slattery. At least, according to the e-mails she'd read. Jonah saw the look on her face and blanched a little, realizing what he had said.

"We all have secrets," Amber said as neutrally as she could—he could take it either as a peace offering or a threat.

"You would have gone with them," Jonah said slowly, realizing.

"I like it here. My baby's safe here. I wish we were all still together." Each of these separate sentences was true. Not strongly true, but true enough for the moment. Jonah cocked his head, studying her, then continued to help her inside.

And as long as he doesn't find out that I actually contacted them—we all will *be together again,* Amber thought, shivering. Maybe they could all go to L.A. with Keely.

She bet it was warm there.

TWENTY-FIVE

Two short squawks and a long one. Michael and Keely rushed over to the walkie-talkie; Diego was out patrolling, covering any stray tracks, listening for intruders. Irene found the waiting time without him nearby almost unbearable. Even with Dr. Gilmore there to distract her with lectures, it was hard to avoid pessimistic thoughts.

We're in the middle of the woods in the middle of the country, waiting for a madman's daughter to signal us that it's okay to come in and save the world.

"What does that mean?" Irene asked as quietly and calmly as she could.

"She's in," Michael explained as Keely signaled back two quick squawks. "So far everything's okay. Next she's going to try to figure out what's happening, what's going on with the virus and her dad's plans. She'll signal us when she's got some info—or something's gone wrong."

"Yay," Irene said weakly.

Great. More waiting.

"Want to talk about smallpox?" Dr. Gilmore asked brightly.

TWENTY-SIX

DINNER WITH UNCLE FRANK AND HER DAD WAS COZY—A LITTLE *too* cozy. With the guards nearby and various polite but gossipy flunkies around, it was as close to a state dinner for publicity as the leader of Novo Mundum could accomplish. Soon, weepy-eyed, the guards and servers would go off shift and tell everyone about how the first family was so happy to be back together.

But Liza was led away from watchful eyes and into her dad's study afterward, alone. In some ways, more alone than she had been waiting outside the gate.

"Where's Uncle Frank going?" she asked as casually as she could. There was an unopened pack of cigarettes on her dad's desk; his equivalent of a worry stone. He smoked once in a *very* great while, where no one could see or smell it, having never entirely kicked the habit—but only when he was at his worst. The sight of the pack made Liza even more uneasy.

"Frank has some missions he needs to set up and send out—nothing you need to worry about. Though we should get you over to Dr. MacTavish's. . . ." He frowned. Liza waited for him to tell her that it was so she could get the Strain 8 vaccine, but he didn't say anything. Instead he sat down in his chair and looked up at her, eyes narrowing slightly. "So. You've had quite the adventure."

"Yeah." Liza threw herself into the chair across from him, like the tired little girl he might remember. If he wanted to play the concerned parent, she would go along with the scenario. "It sucked out there. I am so glad to be back home."

"Tell me again what happened," her father said, leaning forward and pressing his hands together like an understanding preacher.

"I *told* you and Uncle Frank," Liza said, feeling peeved. "They sort of kidnapped me. Michael told me he loved me and it was for my own good. Then later, after Diego stopped the people you sent out after us, we were all captured by the Slash. Then we escaped and they let me go."

"The Slash." Her father's eyes lit up with actual interest—this was safe ground. "Tell me about them."

Liza shuddered, again not pretending. "They took over a zoo. The women are all slaves. The men are all insane. They kill and torture without a thought. And somehow they trained a tiger to hunt for them," she added, frowning. "I don't know how they managed that."

He nodded. "I've had some reports of their activities. Barbaric, though they seem rather well organized."

Liza wondered how much he really knew. Did the Novo Mundum scouts realize that Michael's ex-girlfriend was their queen? She tried not to think of the insane girl they'd left, bloody and laughing. "It was like Novo Mundum in hell."

Her father raised an eyebrow, and she realized those last words weren't ringing Liza-true. She had begun to speak like the others—Michael and Keely and Dr. Gilmore.

"It sounds like you've been through quite an ordeal. How did the others fare? Your friend Michael?"

"He was definitely a lot more dangerous than I ever thought," Liza said, searching her mind for some way to turn the conversation back to Strain 8. Why hadn't he told her yet about the vaccine? About the new plan for keeping Novo Mundum safe? And wasn't he worried about her safety if the virus was going to be released near the campus?

Her father pushed back in his chair and gazed off at the wall, as if relaxing. This was when he was most dangerous, the sleeping tiger, she used to call it. She used to love watching him come at students with a sudden zinger from this angle.

"And why did they let you go afterward?"

"They had no more use for me." Liza shrugged.

"They said I could come with them if I wanted, but screw that. I wanted to come back home."

"Even though Michael asked you to stay."

"He almost got me *raped* and *killed*," Liza said a little shrilly. Did her own father really think she was that much of a pushover? Or was this part of his strategy, to get her worked up and off guard? "And he only brought me along to keep the rest of them safe from you, as a hostage. Why would I want to go along with them?"

"I don't know." Her father squinted as if it were an interesting hypothetical question. "Why would you?"

Liza slumped in her chair, trying not to let her mind become defeated and exhausted. She couldn't let him get answers out of her, twist her into believing him again. She was the only obstacle between him and her friends, the only person who had a chance of preventing more death and devastation.

It was going to be a very long night.

TWENTY-SEVEN

AMBER PICKED AT HER BOILED BITTER GREENS AND TRIED NOT to frown. Normally it wouldn't have taken a lot of effort, but in her current pregnancy phase all food was good. Especially anything savory, and there was definitely salt and garlic in there. *Why, oh, why, couldn't* anyone else *have come back?*

Liza sat in the chair next to her bed, exhausted and depressed. It was a new look for her.

"Oh, and Diego and Irene shared a room in Texas," the girl added after a moment, a tiny spark in her eye. That was interesting, at least.

"Have they done it?" Amber tried to make the appropriate gesture with her hips, but even something as simple as that was now hard—and sometimes made her dizzy.

"I don't know. Probably." She changed the subject quickly. "Hey, how's your—what was it? Preeclampsia?"

Wow, she actually remembered. Was Liza always basically a decent human being and Amber had never noticed, or had this trip turned her into a more grown-up Dorothy? Probably the latter.

"It sucks," Amber said, grimacing. "I mean, I got all fainty trying to see you. As long as I stick to the bed or move *very slowly,* it's fine. And the baby's fine. You can hear her heartbeat now."

"It's a girl?" Liza asked excitedly.

"Um, I don't know. No sonograms or stuff like that." Amber blushed at being caught out. "I just—kinda hope. I'm sort of sick of guys. We need more women in the world now, I think."

"Amen to that," Liza said.

Hmm, maybe things between Liza and Michael weren't so peachy anymore?

"You okay?" Amber asked, more concerned about the other girl than she would like to have admitted to herself.

Liza stood up and began pacing, clenching and unclenching her fists. "It's been over a day—almost *two* days now and Dad hasn't sent me in to get the vaccine or even told me about it. Like I'm not going to find out from everyone else here how you all got shots?"

"That *is* a little weird," Amber agreed, nodding slowly. She didn't want to say the first thing that leapt to mind. But from the look on Liza's face, it was obvious that she had thought of it too.

"Maybe he doesn't care," Liza said softly.

"Maybe you'd better watch your back," Amber suggested, a little more coldly than she'd meant to, but it looked like Novo Mundum's prodigal princess could be a little dense sometimes.

TWENTY-EIGHT

LIZA DIDN'T TRUST HER ABILITY TO FOOL ANYONE ANYMORE about "going in to visit Daddy"—especially since he was in command central with Uncle Frank, probably discussing whether or not she had been telling the truth about her little trip and what they should do about it. Like find out if there were others with her. The good news was that they wouldn't go anywhere near the train station in St. Louis and couldn't ask questions of actual citizens. Besides, Uncle Frank had said something about being short-staffed these days. . . .

She tiptoed through the medical building—Amber had told her "the way would be clear," whatever that meant. But all the doors were unlocked, and a hammer had been left conveniently near the planks she had to remove from the door—the ones that had been put across it since their escape. Dr. MacTavish wasn't subtle, but she *was* resourceful.

Because Liza was tiny, she only needed to pry a single plank out and slide it aside. It took *forever* since she wasn't that strong and tried to make as little noise as possible. There really were fewer guards around than usual; someone had mentioned that some were on their way back from a mission. . . . Probably Twin Elms. Liza shivered. Two of the guards she knew had carried out her father's plans to test Strain 8 as a weapon. Did they know what they were doing? How could they live with the consequences?

She carefully hid the hammer and squeezed through, sucking in her stomach and praying that her clothes wouldn't tear and leave a telltale string. The gun, under her belt, caught for a moment, but a twist of the hips and she was on the other side, shoving it more tightly into her waistband. Liza carefully pulled the plank back into place, hung on a single nail she had left exposed.

It was 1 a.m. and everyone was gone. Through the windows she had watched the dying glow of blue artificial lights and orange flames from candles, dim things that wouldn't expose their presence on government satellite. Her dad's scientists and research assistants often worked late into the night, building the world anew—by taking it down first, apparently.

She tiptoed down the hall to the lab her father frequented most, not the one where he spoke to his gathered minions and explained their upcoming tasks, but the smaller one he used as an office, where he used to write papers back when he was just a professor at Greenwich.

Liza's eyes had adjusted enough for her not to bang into furniture; when she got to his desk, she risked using the illuminated face of the McDonald's watch Michael had looted from Irene's aunt's house. There was her father's desk and the drawer that once occasionally hid a candy bar despite her warnings about possible weight gain, now locked shut with a bicycle cable and a combo lock.

It was almost too easy—her mother's birthday, month and year. If it had been Uncle Frank, it probably would have been Liza's own—besides being just more comfortable around her uncle, she was beginning to see the real differences between her real father and her avuncular one.

She pulled the cable out of the lock and reached for the drawer pull . . .

"Liza, what are you doing?"

Standing in the doorway was her father. Like something out of a nightmare—one you have as a kid in which your parents aren't really who you thought they were, monsters in disguise. His voice was almost casual and his hand reached over to flip on the small, shaded light that was screwed onto the wall. Unlike the spotlight the soldiers had shined on her, this illuminated almost nothing except her father's features and the drawer she was about to open.

A thousand lies came to her lips—but none of them

were believable in the slightest. The truth came out instead, and it sounded equally false.

"I'm trying to look for proof that you had nothing to do with what happened at Twin Elms Two."

She forced herself to look up into his eyes—somehow it wasn't fair that she was almost as tall as she was ever going to be, still child size compared to her dad. He would never look up to her or even directly into her eyes. Her heart pounded so badly it was missing beats.

Dr. Slattery just shook his head, keeping his eyes on her.

"Don't you think *you're* the one who has some explaining to do?"

Fear gave way to frustration. He had asked a simple question—she had answered it. Instead of addressing the issue he'd changed the subject, making it about her. She had always been irritated a little by the way he smoothly deflected things that he didn't want to talk about, but she had never figured out how to get around it. Her first urge was to answer—*No!* she had explained enough already. But something new inspired her: stick to the subject.

"Did you have anything to do with what happened at Twin Elms Two?" she asked as calmly as she could.

"Why did you run away?" her dad asked back, sighing and putting his hands into his lab coat pockets, defeated. "Don't you like it here? Isn't it safe? Is it *me* you were running away from?"

"Dad, I *love* it here," Liza said, biting her lip—she *had* abandoned her father, who did love her, whatever else he might be involved in. "And compared to what I've seen outside—I love it more than ever." Dr. Slattery's eyes widened very slightly at this. "I think what you've done here is great. I'm just now beginning to understand the sort of brains and hard work it took to make Novo Mundum happen." *And strong will and charismatic personality.* Cult leader attributes, as Keely had suggested. He certainly knew how to manipulate people. . . .

"It *was* hard work. It still is. We're stronger than ever but still unprepared against every eventuality." He was obviously pleased with what she had said, but a moment later his face relaxed again into that scary impassivity. "You're not answering my question, though, Liza."

"And you're not answering mine," she shot back. *"Did you have anything to do with what happened at Twin Elms Two?"*

"Liza, I know you had your little Patty Hearst moment there, running away with the cool kids—but I am your *father.*" He walked toward her, managing to look both angry and disappointed at the same time. Liza flashed back to when she had accidentally broken a vase—and then hidden the pieces under the sink. She knew it would have been fine if she had just come clean but hadn't been able to bring herself to do it. The punishment—no TV for a week—had been a lot easier to bear than the moments when her dad first found out and suddenly appeared, looming over her. "I do not have to answer your questions—*you* have to answer mine."

"Dad, I'm *sixteen*—that's more than grown up in the rest of the world now!" Liza cringed as soon as she spoke the words. He was drawing her in again, making it a fight between them, a family thing. Not about killer viruses and deadly electric fences. She took a step backward. "Over three hundred people were living there—they didn't do anything to anyone. They were just like Novo Mundum—harmless people trying to survive and rebuild a better world!"

"We can talk about this at length if you want, Liza," he said, taking another step forward. "But first you have to settle down and behave. Tell me the *truth* about your friends—and why they let you come back."

Ah, the carrot. Liza tried to ignore the rush of relief she felt at the peace offering and the hopeful look in his eye. He was being both good and bad cop at the same time.

"I think you're more concerned about protecting Novo Mundum than you are about me," Liza said, forcing the words out. "Ever since I got back, you've been questioning me like a prisoner—you haven't really acted that pleased to see *me,* your own daughter. And you didn't even ask how I was or how they treated me! Just the story, over and over again, to see if I was lying . . ."

"Honey, I was worried sick the entire time you were gone—the days you were missing, I spent in agony. I just want to know exactly what happened and how you managed to come back to me."

"Back to *you?*" Liza shouted, suddenly overcome with rage. "Do you even care about me? *Why haven't you given me the same vaccine you gave to everyone else?*"

Dr. Slattery's face went blank with surprise—for just a moment.

"Of course I will," he said, trying not to stutter. "But you're probably immune. . . . That's why I wasn't so worried. Of course I love you and worry about you, Liza. You're my only girl. Come on, we'll do it now. *I'll* do it. Will that prove to you how much I love you?"

He put his hand out, a sad but hopeful look on his face.

Liza stared. A memory flashed through her mind. When she was younger and it was cold out, he never yelled at her for forgetting her mittens; he would take off his own glove and wrap her hand in his.

Was he serious? Who knew? She didn't anymore.

And she hesitated too long.

His long arm closed the gap between them faster than she was prepared for, and he grabbed her left hand in his solid, fatherly grip.

Before Liza knew what she was doing, she pulled out of his grasp. He made another reach for her—more violently; anger had begun to show on his face. The true face of the monster was finally beginning to show itself. In some ways, it was a relief.

She pulled out the gun.

Her father looked at it, shocked for a moment, then smiled. *Mistake!* He made her so angry she almost pulled the trigger right then and there. "You're not going to shoot me."

"I guess a man who loves his little social experiment more than his own daughter wouldn't think twice about killing an entire community to protect it," she said, trying to focus. It was hot. Her hand shook. Where did she go from here? What now? What was the possible ending to this situation?

"Liza, I always hoped you would stop being such a silly little girl—what is it you kids call it? 'Drama queen'? This"—he indicated the gun and her in one wave—"is just another sign of your immaturity and possible mental instability. Maybe if you'd had a mother growing up, things would be different."

Things were slipping, going out of control. Already she was questioning herself: Was she insane? Pointing a loaded gun at her father? What the hell was wrong with her? *Must focus!*

"Did you unleash Strain 8 on Twin Elms Two?" Liza demanded, gesturing with the gun.

Her father looked at her for a long moment, as if making a difficult decision. She could practically see the neurons firing desperately behind his eyes.

"Yes," he finally said, looking down at the ground for a moment as if he was the smallest bit ashamed.

Everything Keely and Michael and Irene and Diego said was true. Liza was stunned—she hadn't expected so exact an answer so coolly stated. Some sort of explanation was more her dad's way—a lecture on the need to protect Novo Mundum, the value of lives in a post–Strain 7 world. How this place was humanity's last best hope for survival of the mind.

She swallowed, trying to decide which question to follow it up with.

"Did—"

Before she could continue, Dr. Slattery brought his hands up. They hadn't actually been *in* his coat pockets, just hovering right outside them—she saw that now. He grabbed her wrist and held it tightly, squeezing until she felt her bones rub up against each other. She brought her left hand down over and over again on his hands, but they wouldn't budge.

"I think you and I need to have a little talk. In the quarantine room."

"No!" Liza twisted and turned, but he forced the gun down, aiming it at the floor. *"Murderer!"* she screamed.

"I'm sorry I have to do this." He almost sounded sincere. "Your uncle is going to be devastated."

A dim memory came forward, from when they'd been attacked by the Slash, something from the self-defense class she took at Greenwich. Liza let herself fall to the ground, a deadweight, prepared to kick him with her legs.

"Liza . . . !" her father yelled, angry now. He released one of his hands to grab her shoulder. . . .

And the gun went off.

Just like that.

The trigger was already partially squeezed—the release of his left hand caused it to fall farther, pulling it the rest of the way. Her ears rang and she felt dizzy. She looked up.

Her father's face was wrenched in shock, that expression she'd seen on TV victims who had just been unexpectedly shot. *It's real,* Liza noted dreamily as her father opened his mouth once or twice. Nothing came out. Not even blood—which was a little surprising. He let her go and clutched his stomach, staggering backward, still trying to say something.

Then he fell.

He curled up in a fetal position, clutching his stomach, and died with his eyes open.

Liza pushed herself back along the floor, away from the corpse. She stared at the very literally smoking gun in her hand, then at her father's body beyond it. Everything seemed quiet, slow, frozen, black and white, except for the circle of blood that gently and brightly enlarged itself.

"What the hell is going on in here—?"

Frank Slattery threw himself into the room, a gun in one hand. He stopped, arms falling to his sides, when he saw the scene in front of him.

"Uncle Frank . . . ?" Liza whispered, feeling the first stirrings of confusion.

"Oh God, Liza . . ." Her uncle's craggy, harsh features became a mask of dismay and sadness. He put a hand to his forehead. For the first time ever in her life, it seemed like he didn't know what to do.

"He—he was going to take me to the quarantine room," she stammered. "I was hoping everyone was wrong. . . ."

"You shouldn't have come back," he repeated weakly.

"He just . . . admitted to killing everyone in Twin Elms. With his virus," she said, trying to look at the gun in her hands, but her eyes focused inward, saw the scenes from TV. The bodies.

"I was almost—*almost*—relieved when you left. I wish they had left without you. They're going to *kill you*," he added, suddenly turning to look at her and not his brother's body. It was true; she could hear shouts in the distance. Probably everyone was wondering where Frank was.

"I just shot my own father," Liza said, feeling something like regret. Huge, individual racking sobs came up from her belly and stung her throat. The urge to vomit was almost uncontrollable.

"Liza, listen up." Uncle Frank shook his head and hardened his face, snapping back into action like he usually did. "I'm going to fire another shot in the air. You start screaming, you hear me? When they come in, I'm going to run away, and you're going to tell them that *I* shot Paul. Do you understand?"

Liza looked up at him slowly, hearing the words but not grasping their meaning.

"I'll take the blame!" he said desperately. "They'll *kill* you otherwise! Liza girl, pull it together!"

He strode forward and put his hand out. She timidly held it and he pulled her to her feet. "You gotta take over now, you understand? Think on your feet. Tell them I was jealous or something and you came in, tried to stop me. Okay?"

Finally the tears came and Liza began to cry.

He pulled her in for a last, tight hug and mussed the top of her hair with the hand that wasn't holding the gun.

"I'm sorry, Uncle Frank," she sobbed.

"*I'm* sorry, Liza girl. For . . . so many things." He gently pushed her back and away, giving her one more squeeze on the shoulders. "Remember. Think on your feet."

She nodded and he raised his own gun to the ceiling, closed his eyes, and fired.

Liza began screaming. Screeching, not like when she wanted to be let back into Novo Mundum. Like the world was falling apart and someone was attacking her and the worst nightmarish shapes had invaded her room. It didn't take a lot of effort.

A couple of guards finally took action; she heard them pounding up the stairs as her uncle mouthed *goodbye* at her. She raised her gun at him and he tensed to run.

"Sir—what's going on here?" That was Mario again—he was confused, looking back and forth between him and Liza, training his gun more on her. Then he noticed the corpse on the floor. "Oh my God— Dr. Slattery!"

"He shot my daddy!" Liza wailed, pointing. "He killed him! *Why*, Uncle Frank?"

Mario turned his gun, confused, on his superior.

"He didn't know what he was doing. It was time someone stepped in who did," he said harshly. It sounded a little fake to Liza's ears—he wasn't the sort of person who was used to lying—or at least hadn't developed it as a smooth talent, like her father.

"Sir?" the guard asked. "I think—I think I have to place you under arrest," he said uncertainly. "Until we get this all sorted out." Wide tears flowed out of his eyes, but he didn't blink. Liza was amazed, as always, just how much other people cared about her father, how devoted they were to him.

"Forget it, kid." Frank took careful aim and shot. The guard dropped his gun arm immediately, his shoulder gushing blood.

Then Frank turned around and ran.

One of the other guards was on the walkie-talkie. "We've got a man down in the labs—confusing situation—we need backup. Going after armed—ah, armed Frank Slattery. All units to lab."

"He *shot* me," Mario murmured, sinking to the floor and cradling his arm. "Why did Colonel Slattery shoot *me?*"

"*Wait!*" Liza cried, trying to think quickly through all of the distractions. She had to give her uncle time to escape—it was the least she could do. "Someone needs to help him." She pointed at her father. They didn't know he was already dead. "We need to get him to the clinic."

The guard looked at her, eyes flickering with indecision for a split second, then nodded. He went back to the walkie-talkie and gave everyone new orders. More soldiers came, more talk on the radios. Dr.

Slattery was put on a gurney—like the one Diego had been strapped into—and rushed to the medical building.

And Liza just stood there, thinking about how her entire family was gone now.

Because of her.

TWENTY-NINE

EVERYONE WAS LIGHTLY DOZING EXCEPT FOR KEELY, WHO HAD watch—and was trying to pick the seeds out of pinecones. That's what pine nuts were, right? And she used to love them on pesto pizzas. . . .

Then the radio crackled.

"Pick up," said a voice over it, crackled and broken up—but definitely feminine. "Somebody pick up."

Diego and her mom were instantly awake, Michael a moment later. Irene slowly sat up on one arm, blinking. Was that Liza? Why was she *speaking?* The one imperative thing was keeping radio silence. . . . Keely grabbed the bright green-and-yellow walkie-talkie and gave the secret signal back, two short blips, pause, then a long one.

"Yeah, yeah," the voice said irritably, tiredly. She

gave the right signal back. "It's Liza. Just pick up the phone. Everything's changed here."

Michael jumped out of his bedroll and went to grab the radio—Keely swiped it away. *Typical Michael, still trying to play the hero.* "What's going on?" she asked Liza carefully.

Michael looked annoyed but chastised. *What happened to radio silence?* he mouthed.

I'm trying to find out, dumb ass! Keely mouthed back.

"Everything—changed. My dad is dead. I—Uncle Frank shot him."

Michael and Keely blinked at each other. Now, *this* was a development no one had expected.

"Frank—gone now," the voice on the radio crackled. "Escaped. No one ruling the roost."

"How did this happen?" Keely asked clearly and slowly.

"Explain later. Sending—people—open fence at gate for you."

"Wait, why should we trust her?" Dr. Gilmore demanded from the background.

Keely stared at the radio, frustrated. She realized her mom was jaded and could very well be right about Liza's treachery. But Keely wanted to trust the girl.

"They might have a gun to her head," Diego pointed out. "Or maybe her dad convinced her."

"Liza . . ." Keely said, holding the talk button down. Michael glared at her, but she winced back. "If she's telling the truth, there's no point to radio silence."

Speaking into the radio, she asked, "How do we know we can trust you?"

"—don't remember questioning *you* when—almost drowned me in—sewer pipe!" came the angry and snippy answer.

"That's Liza, all right," Michael said, "and she doesn't sound like a hostage." Though everyone in the group knew about his breakup with Liza, it seemed to be the general consensus that Michael was the one who knew Liza best.

There was a long pause as the five exchanged worried looks.

Finally there was another squawk. "—just have to. Trust me. Need to figure out. Dad's journals."

It might have just been the radio and interference, but Liza sounded a lot older and exhausted than the girl Keely remembered toting a family heirloom through the wilds of the Big Empty.

Keely looked past her mother to her circle of friends. Diego was shaking his head, as if this was all a roll of the dice, while Michael seemed resigned to helping Liza. Surprisingly, Irene made the first decisive move.

"Do we have a choice?" she asked.

They still didn't walk up the middle of the road; if they were under a little cover, maybe some of them could escape an ambush. They had to do *something* to protect themselves, feel in control.

Keely fell into step beside her mother, trying to gauge her reaction. Catherine Gilmore had a grit-jawed determination locked onto her face; if she was as scared inside as the rest of them, she hid it completely.

But as the road ended in the now familiar twist of rubble and overgrowth, Keely allowed herself a grain of hope. If it *was* a trap, the Novo Mundum soldiers weren't doing a particularly good job of hiding themselves; five stood around the jury-rigged gate built into the electric fence.

The fence that had been a product of their involvement.

She saw Michael turn his head for just a fraction of a second at the sight, eyes glassy. Keely didn't blame him. She had encountered Gabe's corpse in the emergency clinic, and that was bad enough. Michael had actually seen their friend die at this fence, electrocuted while on a mission to "fix" the electric border.

"It's all right," came Liza's voice over a megaphone—again strong but tired. "You can come forward. I told them the truth about how you were trying to save me from Uncle Frank."

Michael looked back at Keely. What the hell was she talking about? They didn't dare even shrug, afraid that much would give them away. *Play along,* Keely silently willed the rest of the group. It probably didn't matter; Irene, Diego, and her mom didn't look like they were ready to say anything to anyone.

Liza pushed her way in front of the soldiers, who still kept their guns trained on the five of them. "It's okay now, really." She extended a hand, looking somewhat regal but shaken, too. "The guards know about how you helped me find out what Uncle Frank was up to. You were right. He was plotting against Novo Mundum, and I tried to stop him, but I was just too late. He *killed* Daddy. I would have been next."

Keely stared, as if trying to follow the lineage in a bad soap opera. Liza was obviously covering but at least seemed to have the overall chaos under control.

Irene accepted Liza's hand and embraced her in a hug. Without a word, she linked arms with her, Diego flanking Liza's other side, and the three of them moved forward, through the gate, into Novo Mundum.

Michael followed them, eyes ahead, unable to engage the border guards who used to be his friends.

This feels hauntingly familiar, Keely thought as she and her mother followed the group through the gate. No visible adversaries, no gunshots . . . only the unseen enemy, a brand-new killer virus.

Just like old times.

Marching across the campus like ghosts of long lost campers, they followed Liza, who gathered them into her uncle's office.

From the hysterical sobs and scattering groups of Mundians, Keely suspected that the word of Slattery's death was still reverberating over the campus, its impact spreading like the concentric rings on the surface of a pond from a falling stone. In a community where everyone had a purpose and most members fulfilled that with a cheerful attitude, people were suddenly shiftless and angry and lost, as if they had mislaid their assigned tasks. Keely sensed the swell of chaos, the vacant eyes, dark with despair and alienation. *Just like outside. Just like after Strain 7 hit.*

"They're the ones who brought it all on!" one guy sneered as Liza led them across the quadrangle. Another Mundian spat at Keely, shouting, *"Traitor!"* as she did. Fortunately her aim was way off.

But finally they were all in "command central," damp and cold but clean, with some of their hunger abated. Liza threw herself wearily into her uncle's chair. There were shadows on her brow and bags under her eyes; she looked years older all of a sudden. *What could have happened in less than a week?*

"We have to be quick about this. Captain Tabori nosy nellie will be here any second demanding to know why she's not in the meeting." She took a deep breath and looked up at them. "*I* shot my dad when he found me in the lab."

They might have had good game faces in front of the soldiers, but even Keely couldn't avoid sucking in her breath. *Liza?* Daddy's little girl? *She* shot Dr. Slattery? Suddenly all of her weariness made sense. How could she do that, though? Keely was torn between shock and incredible sadness. Everyone had wanted Liza to grow up and gain a little maturity—just not this way.

"He tried to grab me," Liza added, as if she needed to explain herself.

"Oh my God, Liza . . ." Michael put his hand out to comfort her.

She pressed her hand against his and squeezed, holding back the pain despite a few tears that sneaked down her cheeks. She swiped them away with her sleeve and continued. "We can talk about all that later. It all went so fast and . . . well, just after the gun went off, Uncle Frank came in and found me and figured out what happened. He made everyone here think *he* did it. To save me."

Wait—the same Frank Slattery who'd had Gabe electrocuted? The same one who might have brought in MacCauley troops just so he could prove a point to his brother? The same one who'd probably fired a rocket launcher at Finch after he exiled himself from Novo Mundum, to keep all secrets safe? Dr. Slattery's partner in crime?

It was weird to think of the bullet-headed army geek as having any feelings at all. People could be a lot more complicated than they seemed, Keely slowly realized.

Liza covered her face with her hands and took a moment to let the tears flow before resuming. Keely felt her own eyes moisten, and Irene also had wet tracks down her cheeks.

"I told everyone—all the guards—that you guys suspected my uncle of trying to take over Novo Mundum by any means possible and persuaded me to leave with you for my own safety."

"That was incredibly quick thinking," Keely said gently, impressed.

Liza looked up at her blankly for a moment before giving a tired smile. "Thanks. I've had to learn fast."

"What do we do now?" Dr. Gilmore asked the question on everyone's minds. "Have you seen it out there? I don't know what this place was like before, but looks like there's barely controlled widespread panic. A lot of rumors are flying around and it's obvious no one knows what's going on . . . only that their leader is dead."

"*Both* their leaders," Keely pointed out. "Er, at least missing."

"Wait, didn't we come back to stop Dr. Slattery?" Diego asked. "Mission accomplished. Uh—sorry, Liza."

Liza shook her head. "We still don't know what he was doing. Was he planning something else *after* Twin Elms Two? Like spreading it to a wider field, to the entire world? A lot of scouts are still out there, and not just those on gathering missions. *Classified* missions."

"We have to go through his notebooks and talk to his technicians and researchers," Irene said. "Just without his help."

"And we have to get them on our side," Dr. Gilmore pointed out. "We can't just lock them up and torture them." Although from the glint in her mother's eye, Keely wasn't entirely sure that she wouldn't enjoy doing some pretty awful things to scientists who made it their life's work to *develop* biological weapons.

"Liza, it's up to you," Michael said slowly. She blinked, not comprehending. "People here will follow the daughter of their leader—you automatically inherit his leadership and their trust, especially as a grieving close family member."

"What are you talking about?" Liza demanded, but more a statement than a question. Michael was right— the answer was obvious. Liza *had* to take over. Novo Mundum would listen to her. And while she helped reorganize the community, she could give the five of them the resources they needed to figure out what her dad had been up to.

"You'll emerge as the next leader if you let it happen, Liza," Michael said. "Just let yourself think about it, think about what you might accomplish here. I know, you've just gone through the worst trauma of anyone's life, and nothing can undo that. But you can turn this place around so that it's not all wasted. Stay on all the *good* things your father wanted to do. It was a nice idea to start again, to create a community devoted to art and literature, safe from the government and the rest of the world. You can continue that dream—without the violent things your father was planning."

"I . . . I can't lead anything . . ." Liza said slowly. "You all *know* that."

"That was before," Keely said. "And something tells me we didn't know you very well at all."

Liza looked down at the floor again. Silence reigned in the room. No one wanted to interrupt her thoughts; no additional words heaped on could have added to Michael's argument.

Please, Keely wished, unconsciously fingering Bree's necklace, *please please please* . . .

The door burst open and Captain Tabori came in. She looked around uncertainly for a moment, then turned to Liza.

"We need to talk," she said bluntly.

This was a problem. Tabori was second in line to Frank, and though she looked grief stricken, she obviously had it more together than Liza. Did she really believe the story about her superior? Did she still feel loyal to him regardless of what he might have done? It was hard to tell anything from her hard, light blue eyes. They were either cold or perpetually angry—and right now Keely couldn't tell the difference.

She was a pretty good candidate for seizing leadership too.

"We all need to talk," Liza said slowly. "I need to talk to everyone. We need to have everyone gather in the large auditorium so I can explain exactly what is going on."

"Exactly what *is* going on?" the head soldier demanded.

"I'm going to take over my father's job and carry out all of his original plans for Novo Mundum, and you're going to take over Uncle Frank's job and help me get everything done. Whatever . . . happened between the two of them, I think it would be a fitting tribute."

Ellen Tabori squinted, staring hard at Liza.

Everyone in the room tensed as an unspoken communication transpired between Liza and the soldier. Whether it was a test of wills, a dance of trust, Keely wasn't sure, but the two women seemed lost in their own universe for that moment.

"Yes, ma'am," Tabori finally said, saluting. "I think that would be an appropriate memorial."

"Good." Liza sighed wearily, giving voice to the general sentiment in the room.

"What should I tell the troops for now? Carry on their routine missions?"

"Absolutely. Now, let's get that town hall under way."

THIRTY

IRENE WAS BACK.

Jonah's heart *definitely* skipped a beat when he first heard the news.

It wasn't a complete surprise. He didn't know a whole lot about Liza beyond what everyone else did—that she was Dr. Slattery's little girl, who maybe helped him run the place, maybe not—but he was pretty sure she couldn't have come back across the wilderness by herself. He was surprised that anyone had believed her. Maybe they'd just wanted to.

How much did Amber really know about all this? If he had been even a little bit nicer to her in the past, would she have told him about everyone returning?

Was Irene still with Diego?

Jonah was supposed to go on that special mission soon—whenever Tabori ordered it. But he still had time to go find Irene and talk to her. Find out what happened. Explain why he'd done what he did.

But did he want to?

How did you bring up *anything* with a person who obviously liked a guy who was willing to shoot you? They clearly had completely different opinions about Novo Mundum and Dr. Slattery, and nothing was going to change that. Not even bullets, apparently. But then why had she come back?

Dr. Slattery . . .

Jonah still hadn't recovered from his death, any more than anyone else at NM had. Maybe less. He'd never had a feeling one way or the other about Frank, but Paul had been . . . everything that was right about Novo Mundum. Its people. The future. *Jonah's* future.

Jonah liked everyone there, and it felt good to have an actual purpose in life, to be needed—it just didn't seem as important without the man who had gone out of his way to take Jonah under his wing. It would take a lot of time to heal from the death of the only person besides his old shop teacher who had really acted like a father to him.

He was *so* not ready to deal with this. Any of this.

Jonah shook his head and shouldered his bag. Nope. He would deal with Irene when he got back. A couple of days by himself away from Novo Mundum would definitely clear his head and give him time to mourn. He pulled out his orders so he could begin mentally preparing the route. Things with his hands and head he could easily figure out. Directions and orienteering and landmarks in nature—not so much.

And they wanted to send him through the deepest part of the unmarked forest.

Jonah sighed. Was *nothing* easy?

THIRTY-ONE

AMBER TWISTED AND TWITCHED IN HER SEAT, SAT WITH HER legs sprawled apart. If it was this bad now, what was it going to be like in the month before the baby was born? She shouldn't complain, though; it was surprising anyone let her come to the big meeting at all. She had managed to make it over in one piece thanks to a wheelchair and extra help. Amber had been more than polite when the nurse had asked if she could sit with her friends. . . .

There was Keely! Waving to her! God, it had only been a few weeks, but it felt like years. Who was that woman with her? Amber found herself waving back, a giant grin spreading across her face. Keely came running, dragging the woman by the hand behind her.

"Oh my God, Amber! Wait—don't get up." Keely

leaned over and hugged her as well as she could. Amber was a little embarrassed by the display but found herself squeezing back. It was amazing how actually happy she was to see her roommate and travel companion again. . . . She was even disappointed when she heard they were back and no one had come to visit immediately, maybe even a little hurt. There were a lot of other things going on, but—well, at least Keely was here now. That was what was important. Amber had never considered herself an educated person, but she hadn't had a decent conversation with anyone since she had left. Keely might be a grind, but at least she had a brain.

"Amber, this is my mom," Keely introduced, indicating the diminutive woman next to her. "Mom, this is Amber."

"Hey." She knew that's who it had to be from what Liza had told her, but it was still meeting the mom in person.

"Nice to meet you, Amber." The older woman smiled—a smile very much like Keely's, several shades of secret away from complete openness, but with a slightly more cynical tilt to it. Mother and daughter carefully stepped around and sat next to her. Amber couldn't help smiling—it felt so good to have her back. "Look, there she is." Keely pointed.

Liza walked out onstage and the murmurs of the crowd rose for a moment, then hushed. She walked with her head bowed, and that butchy Ellen followed her part of the way before stopping to stand at attention to the crowd. *Holy cow, she looks like crap.* Even from this distance it looked like something had been drained out of the princess of Novo Mundum; she looked both thinner and taller at the same time.

When she reached the podium, she looked up.

"Members of Novo Mundum." Her voice was amplified—Amber wondered how the A/V geeks managed that and how it took priority over other things. "There are a lot of questions about what has happened and a lot of talk. I'm here to set things straight. But first, a moment of silence for my father, Dr. Slattery, the founder of Novo Mundum."

Her voice cracked a little, but when she bowed her head, everyone else in the room did too, making the soft noises of a flock of pigeons folding their wings for the night. Amber and Keely bowed their heads too, but when Amber snuck a look, Keely rolled her eyes. Amber felt the urge to giggle for the first time in a long time.

"Thank you." Liza took a deep breath. "Yesterday at 1:07 a.m. Frank Slattery shot his brother in the stomach, killing him." There was a collective sucking in of breaths, mutters and whispers in the crowd as people confirmed or denied what they had heard. "Apparently he had problems with the way my dad was running things . . . and had threatened him on several occasions. I didn't want to believe it. Everyone here knows how much I loved my uncle." She allowed a very sad smile to flicker out over the audience. *Nice.* "My friends tried to warn me, but I wouldn't listen. Finally I had to escape with them, before my uncle could use me as a hostage. They saved my life." Her voice went gravelly as she emphasized this last fact. "Michael, Keely, Irene, Diego, please stand up so everyone can recognize you."

Keely looked at Amber, alarmed, but rose.

"These aren't traitors or deserters—they are heroes, although they had to lie to everyone to get me out. Sorry about that, Amber," she added, managing to pick her out in the crowd. Keely sat down and it was Amber's turn to be alarmed as everyone looked at her, but she just shrugged and nodded.

"It is imperative, now more than ever, to keep my father's dream alive," Liza said, curling her hand into a fist and slowly striking the podium. "Novo Mundum will become a living testament to his ideals, a memorial for his hope in humanity. I will take over where he left off, and together we will work to put this behind us, with a clear eye to the future."

"That kind of sucked," Amber couldn't help whispering to Keely.

"The plebes love it," Keely whispered back, gesturing around at the audience, some of whom were crying. While Amber wasn't *exactly* sure what a plebe was, she got the basic gist.

"Everyone loves to a follow a leader—even one without a penis, I guess."

Keely had to push her fist into her mouth to keep from giggling.

"Shhh!" her mom hissed.

Amber instantly felt chagrined—weird, she didn't even know this woman.

THIRTY-TWO

"OH MY GOD—IRENE! I WAS WONDERING WHEN I'D GET TO see you!"

The normally gruff Dr. MacTavish pulled her into a bear hug—strange, considering how she was all sinew and bones, not beary at all—that almost crushed Irene's collarbone.

Everything still looked the same at the clinic, except for the disturbing buckets of bleach and needles that were balanced everywhere in the back room, soaking.

This reunion was going the way Irene had hoped. Ever since they realized they had to go back, Irene had imagined a thousand different versions of what would happen when she saw her dad, a thousand different things she could say and a thousand different responses. He'd been so *angry* when she had suggested that maybe Novo Mundum wasn't completely the best thing in the entire universe and that Dr. Slattery wasn't some sort of messiah. Her leaving was a betrayal of the family, in his eyes.

But he and Aaron were nowhere to be found— probably out on a scouting mission. Maybe they were looking for her. Wherever they were, their absence kept Irene's stomach wound up and tight. *No closure there.*

"What're all those needles for . . . oh," she realized. "Vaccination injections."

"Yeah." The doctor crossed her arms, instantly grumpy again. "What's going on, really? What's the plan?"

What a strange thing, having an adult, a real doctor, ask *her.*

"Keely brought her mom—she's a virologist, like Dr. Slattery. I guess they even knew each other. We're going through his journals and communiqués to figure out what the big plan was."

"Is," Dr. MacTavish corrected, a worried look on her face. "Whatever it was, at least some of it's been implemented—everyone here has been vaccinated against something."

She didn't have to elaborate, furrowing her brow in worry. Neither Irene, Michael, Keely, Diego, or Dr. Gilmore had been vaccinated—probably not Liza, either.

"Has anyone died from the vaccinations?" Irene asked, wishing she didn't have to.

The doctor shook her head. "Surprisingly, no. Two children got incredibly sick, coming down with symptoms that Dr. Slattery refused to elaborate on but that sound a lot like the first stages of that Strain 8 you told me about. High fevers, joint aches, extreme parching—we had to IV them liquids for a week before they began to recover."

"Nice," Irene said grimly. "I think you'd better come help us out. Leave everything except for emergencies to Chong."

"What about her? She was Slattery's stoolie," the older woman pointed out with a grimace. "Maybe you should question her."

Irene shrugged. "We know she was helping the lab assistants inject patients with Strain 8 and other things—I don't think she actually knew anything other than to keep her mouth shut."

Dr. MacTavish thought about that and then grunted agreement, puttering around the main desk to pick up anything she might need—a notebook, pencil, reading glasses—and throwing them into the pockets of her coat.

"Hey, have you seen Jonah at all?" Irene asked. It had been troubling her since she got back. Not quite as much as the thought of what to say to her dad, but it was something she wanted to get over with. And, if she admitted it to herself, something she was sort of looking forward to. She *did* kind of like Jonah. *If only he wasn't so scared of everything.* She thought she had seen him once—maybe he was avoiding her.

But the doctor just shrugged. "Haven't seen him since I gave him his shot—but that doesn't mean anything. I think he suspects something too; he was awful jumpy and nervous when I did him."

Irene frowned. Amber hadn't seen him around either, but since the two basically hated each other, it wasn't surprising. Still, no one else she asked had seen him recently—where was he?

THIRTY-THREE

HQ WAS SET UP IN A SPARE OFFICE IN THE ALUMNI HALL, CLOSE to where Liza now worked. Michael and Keely read through the communiqués and nonscientific journals kept by Frank and his brother; Dr. Gilmore, Irene, and Dr. MacTavish—when she could—looked through the lab notebooks and the papers Liza found in the locked drawer. There was a lot of running back and forth between there and the lab, but since everyone working in the lab had been told to stop whatever they were doing, they were freer to come in and talk about what they knew. Amber reclined on a gurney in the corner, grumbling agreeably about her task: sifting through hundreds—*thousands*—of near indecipherable short-hand e-mails between the two brothers and their minions in the weeks leading up to the Twin Elms Two incident.

If so much didn't depend on what they were doing—*possibly* the fate of the Western world, depending on how grandiose or mad Dr. Slattery's schemes were—it would actually have been kind of fun. *I guess this is what college would have been like,* Michael mused, looking around the room. Dr. Gilmore could have been a grad student or TA or something and the rest of them just students, trying to finish a project or research assignment together. It was strange working completely as a team, all equals, no superiors.

Michael rubbed his eyes and tried to get back into what he was reading. It just didn't make any sense, though. . . .

11/22

~~Valdes~~ *Hakata, Jabbers, Sosa, Ronson under Robeire, 12–3 o'clock Mitchell, Abrams, Flood, and Noonan under Tabori, 4–7 o'clock Diettrich Hammel Rosenberg Jonah under Chan. Water Robeire, 3, Tabori 1, Chan, 4*
Reread re: Tular

11/29

Affirmative on effects w/detainees
ready to Repeat w/actual

Michael knew about half the people listed fairly well. Why send them at different times? Was Slattery planning a whole lot more missions like Twin Elms—all at different times so it looked random? Paul Slattery might have been a genius scientist, but his brother "the military strategist" wrote like a nine-year-old with ADHD.

Michael's stomach clenched and rumbled. Usually nervousness didn't affect him this badly, but he had hardly been able to keep anything down since being back.

The door opened and Liza came in, looking less tired than she had yesterday but still overwhelmed.

"How're things going in here?"

"Not too bad, making progress . . ." Dr. Gilmore shot him a dirty look but didn't say anything. "What about you?"

"Ech. All afternoon I was meeting with the supplies, growth, and green committees." Liza threw up her hands disgustedly. "We're trying to plan our growth strategy for the next couple of years—and our food supply for the next decade. My father was a frickin' genius. He could hold all of these numbers and thoughts and things in his head, keep everyone balanced and calm. I can't do this!"

"Of course you can," Michael said, reaching out and squeezing her hand. He really believed it, too. Under pressure, Maggie had exploded like a rotten egg. Liza had definitely grown into the task, showing intelligence and resources no one had realized she possessed. He and Diego had worked closely with Liza at first—Michael applying his logistical skills and Diego contributing his survival skills. But now the research team needed them more and Liza definitely seemed to be needing him less. "Did you come up with any ideas? For the food supply?"

"A few," she admitted. Everyone looked at her expectantly. "We need more cows."

"Steak: it's not just for dinner anymore," Keely said, grinning.

"Hey, where's Diego?" Liza asked, sounding more curious than genuinely interested.

"He's in sick bay." Irene jerked her thumb in the general direction. "Vomiting up a storm. Poor guy! He gets sick every time we come here."

"Me too," Dr. Gilmore said, wincing. "I've been having—uh, tummy troubles all morning."

"Maybe it's all the bloody rabbits we've been eating," Michael muttered.

"Welcome to my world," Amber snapped.

"Listen to this," Keely said suddenly, looking up from some of Frank's strategy notes. "'Note: Tell supplies to outfit Valdez and Smith with whatever they need for trip—think ten days, max. Get them vacced first. Pick up munitions from Paul tomorrow.'"

"Valdez and Smith?" Amber asked, looking up. "Those were mentioned in the e-mail I read—right before I warned you guys. They were the ones being sent out to Twin Elms Two. On November eleventh."

"We should go talk to them—see what they know," Keely said.

"I'll send someone to get them immediately," Liza agreed.

"Wait a minute. . . ." Dr. Gilmore scrabbled around through the thin blue books she was looking at, flipping pages. "Aha!" She tapped it. "'Refine 30 ccs 8, fill four sterile glass test tubes. Cork and wax top. By Tues., Nov. 10th.'"

"Yayy," Keely drawled, a little sarcastically, a little like Amber. "We can now prove that the entire community of Twin Elms Two was killed by the hands of a man who's already dead."

"Jesus Christ—he salted the frigging *earth*," her mom said disgustedly, throwing her papers down.

"What's that?" Amber asked.

"Sometimes when Rome sacked a city, like Carthage, they then raked salt into the earth to poison it," Keely explained. "It lasted for generations—nothing could grow there."

How horrible, but clever, Michael thought. Like biological warfare before anyone had thought up a name for it.

Wait a moment. . . .

"Oh my God—" Michael said suddenly, riffling through the last pages he had read.

"What?" Keely demanded. "So I took five years of Latin. Big deal. It's great for the SATs. . . ."

Hakata, Jabbers, Sosa, Ronson under Robeire, 12–3 o'clock

"'Mitchell, Abrams, Flood, and Noonan under Tabori, 4–7 o'clock.'" Michael read it aloud, fighting back panic. "Those aren't the times at which he sent out each troop—they're points on a compass!" He put the note on the table so everyone could read. "Twelve noon is north, three o'clock is east—one person sent out for each 'hour' of the quadrant. . . ."

"They've already done it," Keely whispered. "They went out and spread the virus all around Novo Mundum already—on the twenty-second. Right after we left."

The next entry only confirmed that the virus was alive and worked. *Affirmative on effects w/detainees.* More sick, infected prisoners in Slattery's quarantine unit.

"Uh . . ." Irene coughed nervously. Michael looked up and saw Dr. Gilmore and Keely looking into each other's eyes, practically the same eyes, mother and daughter coming to the same worried conclusion. "Diego? In the infirmary? Vomiting his guts out . . . ?"

Oh, hell.

Trying to save the world from Strain 8, Dr. Gilmore, Keely, Liza, Diego, Irene, and Michael had traveled hundreds of miles just to wind up literally in the middle of it. They had all been exposed—were still *being* exposed—to the deadliest disease the world had ever seen.

THIRTY-FOUR

"First things first," Keely said slowly, recovering before anyone else did. Sometimes it was good to be left-brainy, practical and logical in the face of something too horrible to think about. "Let's go to the infirmary. We can see how Diego's doing and get ourselves checked out and ask the doctor what she knows. Maybe we can still get the vaccine or something. Mom—does it say anywhere that the symptoms of Strain 8 include vomiting?"

Her mother shook her head. "Not specifically—there are notes about the blackened skin, the mucus, the parching, nothing about vomiting. But that might not rule it out: many flu-like viruses have nausea associated with them."

"You okay?" Michael asked Liza, who was staring straight ahead of her in shock.

"*That's* what he meant about not coming back," she murmured. Then she looked up. "When I first saw Uncle Frank, he told me I shouldn't have come back. He whispered it so Dad couldn't hear."

"Why would he take the rap for you if he thought you were infected—and as good as dead?" Dr. Gilmore asked. Keely winced. The downside of too much left brain was an occasionally too cold take on life.

"Maybe to give me hope." Liza shrugged.

"Or maybe he figures Liza is naturally immune," Michael suggested.

Catherine Gilmore cocked her head at him. "That's a stretch. I guess you can always hope."

"Yes," Liza said, letting out a breath, as if she had to give up things she could not control. A new deep breath and once again she was focused, pulling herself together. "I—can't go with you," Liza said, as if thinking aloud. "I have to send for those two guards—Valdez and the other guy. Not to mention two more meetings this afternoon. One to deal with planning out our next scouting mission. We need more surgical supplies," she added with an ironic smile.

Keely was amazed. This girl—like the rest of them— had just been told she had been exposed to an incurable, deadly virus, and she was about to go do work. True, there was nothing she could do to help, but it was a far cry from the Liza Slattery that Keely had first met.

Keely stepped forward and touched Liza lightly on

the arm. "We'll meet up later and compare notes," Keely said.

Liza nodded. "And update me if anything breaks for you." Then she left.

"I don't want to be all selfish, but am I all right? And my baby?" Amber asked. Although she sounded tough, Keely could see her keeping her eyes wide open and not blinking—a surprisingly youthful trick for not crying she'd never expected to see on her street-kid roommate.

"You're fine," Keely's mom said, swallowing back the "probably." "Keely—you and Irene go talk to that Dr. MacTavish. I'm going to go back to the lab and look through Slattery's other notebooks, maybe talk to one of the technicians. See if they can help us out with anything."

Keely nodded. No such thing as miracle cures; she knew that from being the daughter of one of the country's top virologists. Most of it was letting the body heal itself in the optimum conditions—lying down, lots of hot soup and fluffy pillows. Making sure no secondary infections set in. Of course, there was always a chance that they were "naturally immune," the way they were against Strain 7—or maybe strong enough to recover.

The wolfish thoughts at the gate of Keely's mind didn't really count that as a possibility, though.

"Come on," Irene said, walking dazedly through the door. "Let's go."

They hadn't even put on their jackets, but Keely didn't feel the cold. It was more like a nuisance when the wind blew, forcing itself up in her arms and into her neck. In the still air it was just *there,* something present and even a little painful but nothing to be really concerned about. The campus was dressed perfectly for an end-of-the-world scenario: thick gray snow; endless, undifferentiated thick gray clouds; the strange light that hadn't changed in days. It was getting on toward dusk; shadows seemed to be darkening as they walked.

One huddled group of Mundians hurried from the warmth of the forge in the shantytown next to the dining hall; the little candle they carried with them more for cheer than heat or light blew out in a sudden slap of wind.

How appropriate.

Irene was far ahead, finally picking up speed with some urgency in her own head—whatever was happening with Diego, it had already been decided by fate— didn't she realize that?

Suddenly Keely felt very alone; she had visions of the virus showing itself like in a science-fiction movie, glowing black and purple as it flowed through her bloodstream.

"I really," Michael began out of nowhere, *"really* don't want to die."

Kelly turned to look at him, surprised.

"I realize it's a little late to decide this," he continued with a faint smile, "what with Strain 7, running away from the government, getting shot at by the guards here and captured by the Slash there. . . . I don't know, maybe it's *because* of all those things. Too many brushes with death. I just . . . really don't want to die."

It was almost clichéd how Keely's own panic disappeared in the face of another's fear; she was still scared, but not alone in it. And someone needed her, pulling her out of herself.

"Me neither," she agreed. "But we're not dead yet. C'mon. We've got work to do—and I refuse to believe we traveled several thousand miles back and forth to end up in hospital beds." With a grin she took his hand in her own and started walking again toward the clinic, pulling him along.

Michael rolled his eyes. "You're *so* going to be disappointed, Gilmore. . . ." But he squeezed her hand and followed, trying to hide a smile of his own.

It was just as cold and windy as at the beginning of their walk, but when the gusts hit her, Keely felt like now she had more substance, that she was more of a rock against the storm.

Never had the ugly fluorescent lighting of the waiting room appear sadder or scarier; the last time she'd been in it was to mourn over Gabe's dead body. Irene was already far inside, clasping Diego's hand and talking to him softly. Dr. MacTavish stood, arms crossed, a look of angry puzzlement on her face.

"I cannot *believe* this," she said, scowling.

Keely sighed and threw herself into a chair. "Want to look at our tongues, tonsils, or whatever? See if we've got something fatal?"

"Uh, where's the bathroom?" Michael suddenly asked. He looked nervous, and his forehead was popping out sweat beads like popcorn.

"Over there—but you can use one of these pans to vomit. . . ." Before the doctor could finish her sentence, Michael had spun and gone. Keely found herself cracking a smile, even in the midst of everything. "Seems more like stomach flu to me," the older woman muttered, pulling out an instrument and turning its light on. She checked down Keely's throat and in her ears, worked her tonsils, and felt her breathe.

Keely didn't think she had ever felt anyone with colder hands before—especially after Michael's nice warm ones.

"Well, you seem fine. For now," she added, sitting back on the desk. "After the—uh—coup, I asked Liza for permission to look in on her dad's victims. . . ." Keely couldn't help sucking in her breath. "You'd be surprised how many were genuinely upset on hearing the news about Slattery. That's some *nice* brainwashing, that is, when you're literally weeping blood for the angel of death."

Keely started to squirm a little. It was nice that the doctor felt she could be so honest and frank with her about the truth, but couldn't she sugarcoat it a *little?* There was a good chance that Keely and all of her friends would be in the same position in a week or so. . . .

"Anyway, *one* of them was one of Slattery's little helpers. He's doing a little better than the others—I was thinking maybe your mom could talk to him. I don't know if he caught it accidentally or if Slattery decided that his help was no longer needed for his little project and the fewer people who knew about it the better. My knowledge of viruses is rudimentary at best, and it sounds like this guy really knows what he's talking about."

"Thanks. I'll tell Mom. You gave *everyone* here the vaccine, right?"

"Yep." The doctor took out a hypodermic needle and shook it. "Or whatever it is. Just joking—I'm pretty sure it's what Slattery said it was. If he was trying to kill us all, well, we'd all be dead by now. Speaking of—you haven't had any symptoms or anything, have you?"

The older woman said it casually, but quietly, so Michael in the bathroom and Diego and Irene couldn't hear. Keely shook her head—and extended her arm, knowing sadly what was going to come next.

Without another word, the doctor reached over and gave her the injection.

"Thanks," Keely said, trying not to wince from the pain.

"I don't know if it's too late, according to what Irene said. But better safe than sorry."

Michael emerged, looking a little sheepish but more like his usual self—if a little paler.

"I don't want to go *that* way," he said, trying to joke. Dr. MacTavish just rolled her eyes.

The double doors flew open, letting wind and a stinging mote of light, papery snow into the room. Dr. MacTavish covered her face and cursed incoherently. A small girl stood there as if she had appeared from out of the snow, a nymph of the storm. Keely realized it was the same girl who'd first led them into Novo Mundum; a hood was pulled over her head against the storm. It was a day of weird omens.

"The savior's daughter needs to see you! Immediately!" she said breathlessly.

"Savior's daugh—? Oh." She meant Liza. Great, already the evil Dr. Slattery had attained a posthumous messianic state.

"Stay out of the snow, you twits!" the doctor snapped. "You're not well. And close that door!"

"Sorry, it sounds serious," Keely apologized. She waved at Irene, who didn't see, too engrossed with Diego. When she and Michael left, following the snow sprite, they didn't hold hands again. Maybe it was because they were headed toward Liza. . . . Michael had told Keely that he and Liza had broken up, and it had sounded final. But still, it was pretty recent. Maybe it felt weird showing up in front of his ex holding another girl's hand?

And wait, was it really a big deal to Keely anyway? She pressed her lips together, trying not to think of the tingles that had radiated up her arm while Michael held her hand in his.

Liza stood behind the big desk when they arrived, looking at something they couldn't see at first. When she heard them come in, she flicked a glance their way and gave a tiny, twitchy smile.

"Please come in," she said, trying to make her voice as low and leader-y as possible. "The situation has now officially become much worse."

All Keely could think about for the first few seconds was the glorious warmth of this inner sanctum; she could feel her fingers and toes finally. Then Michael grabbed her hand, pointing.

Farther in, they could see five heavily armed MacCauley rangers and their leader, in white snow camouflage—all with sleek and enormous guns.

THIRTY-FIVE

"How did they . . . ?" Keely voiced it first, the same thing Michael was thinking.

"Now, that would be telling," the leader of the rangers said, a very slight smile on his face. He wasn't *that* much older than Michael, but he had a large scar on his cheek like an old G.I. Joe doll and his light brown eyes had creases around them, like he had learned and seen too much, too fast.

"It must have been while I was letting you guys in," Liza said tiredly, sitting back down in her chair, as if showing bravery by standing didn't matter anymore. "They've probably been *inside* for the last twenty-four hours."

"Smart girl," the leader said with a grin, but it wasn't patronizing.

"You're all dead," Michael whispered, shaking his head. They had been looking for ways to beat MacCauley soldiers. . . . This wasn't it, though. This wasn't fair.

"That's a pretty ballsy statement there, mister." The leader's smile faded a little and he trained his gun on him and Keely.

Nice one, Michael thought. *Way to go.* The old Michael never would have done that, never screwed up the first verbal volley, first impressions. . . . This guy even looked almost reasonable.

"We found her, sir!"

Another ranger in snow camo—*how many of them were there, anyway?*—pushed Keely's mom into the room, a gun at her back and a big hand over her mouth. The leader looked confused at the use of so much force to restrain the little woman and waved his hand, shaking his head. The ranger shrugged and pulled his hand away.

"You *idiots!*" Dr. Gilmore spat as soon as she could talk. "You bunch of *morons!* You—*chicken-brained biological disasters!*"

Michael saw Keely smile a little. Mother and daughter definitely shared an attitude.

"Dr. Gilmore." The leader saluted her. "We've never formally met, but I've been tracking you since Texas. James Garrison."

Garrison . . . ? That was the name of the colonel in Houston that everyone liked and trusted. The one who let the shops stay open. Was this him? Michael began to feel like he could get a handle on the situation.

"Why didn't you just grab us in the woods? Or *anywhere else for the last thousand miles?*" Keely demanded, sounding exactly like a younger version of her mom. Michael put a hand on her shoulder and shook his head very slightly: *Don't antagonize them.*

"You can't leave now, you know," her mom said, hands on her hips. "*All* of you have been exposed to Dr. Slattery's little October Project—Strain 8."

The otherwise storm-trooper-esque men in camo shifted nervously at that, looking at each other. "You're just saying that. . . ."

"She's not," Michael said calmly. "We can show you all the records we went through. That was the whole reason we were bringing Dr. Gilmore here—to stop Slattery from releasing the virus. But he did. Everyone else here has had a vaccination."

"I think you had better start from the beginning," Garrison said, gesturing with his gun.

It took only an hour and a half. Despite himself, Michael was impressed by Garrison's questions: they were few, directed, and to the point. Liza told the first part, from her perspective, and Michael and Keely took turns telling the rest. When they were done, Liza surprised them all by demanding that Garrison tell them *his* story.

"The government would hardly let one of its last remaining top virologists out of its sight right now," Garrison said, shrugging. "No one had any problem with you going to pick up your daughter and coming home with her—tailed and watched the entire time, of course. When you left Houston to go *north,* my men and I were ordered to follow you."

"Why?" Dr. Gilmore asked. "Why didn't you just take us home *then*—as I believe my daughter asked before?"

"Something very unusual was obviously up with you—we were told to investigate but not to interfere unless it looked like harm was going to come to you or something else dramatic happened. There were rumors of another survivalist camp up here; we figured that was where you were going."

"We are *not* survivalists," Liza said icily. "We're Novo Mundum, and while you all are chasing and shooting civilians, we're trying to *save* civilization."

"Wait, why are you guys so interested in my mom, anyway?" Keely asked before Garrison could respond. She turned to look at her mother. "Your research . . . does this involve biological warfare or something?"

"In a manner of speaking. Can I sit down?" Dr. Gilmore asked, already lowering herself into a chair. Michael had to admire her guts. "This is all defcon 12—or whatever you call top secret. I'm still not used to all this military jargon."

For once Garrison looked worried. "Ma'am, I don't think you should be talking about this in front of them or my men. . . ."

"You're a dead man," Dr. Gilmore gently pointed

out. "Everyone here in this room is. We're not taking secrets anywhere."

The news hit Michael like a rock to the stomach. He had known this, he had been told this earlier, but it still somehow hadn't sunk in. Knowing you had a deadly disease was somehow different from being informed that you were definitely going to die. He tried to quiet his heart, which was suddenly beating out of control—like the panic attacks he used to get as a kid. *Holy crap, I really am going to die,* fought with, *Pull it together, Michael,* but the former was definitely winning.

Then Keely looked at him. The news had struck her the same way, like she hadn't believed it all before. Somehow just knowing that and feeling her hand in his was enough to calm him down. He took a deep breath and refocused on her mom.

"Strain 7 was a virus that arose naturally in the outskirts of Rwanda—forty years ago," she explained. "Because of the remoteness of the villages it struck, the virus didn't spread. Our government obtained a sample—for study or for military purposes, take your pick. Along with a vial of smallpox, a sample of anthrax, and all sorts of other potential biological weapons—or deadly things to be studied, again take your pick—it was stored in a top secret, hidden government vault.

"Two years ago that vault was broken into."

Two years? But that would put it at . . . When the outbreak of Strain 7 began.

"If the government knows who did it, they aren't telling," Dr. Gilmore continued, shrugging. "But whatever group was responsible for the theft—and possibly the deployment—also stole *almost everything else in the room.*"

Stunned silence filled the room.

"Here my dad was spending all this effort trying to create a *new* virus," Liza said bitterly, "and there are *tons* of them out there now of his choosing."

"You were working on vaccines for all of those things," Keely realized.

"That's why you're so valuable to them," Michael chimed in. "*I* wouldn't want anything to happen to you either."

"Too late," Dr. Gilmore said with forced levity.

"Not for us," Garrison corrected. "My men and I stick to the original plan. We bring back Dr. Gilmore and tell the boys in charge about this place. And then they send in people to take it out."

"I cannot *believe* I'm being ordered about by a dead man!" Dr. Gilmore growled.

"You can't leave," Michael repeated firmly. "You pose a risk to the rest of the world."

"I'll radio ahead and tell them that all of us need to be quarantined," Garrison said, raising his gun. "And unless everyone here—and I mean *every*one—evacuates back to the cities quietly, *every*one here is a dead man too."

"With whatever time we have left, we need to continue to figure out what Slattery's plans were, if they even ended here," Keely pointed out. "Obviously he had no trouble testing out his little concoctions on other communities, like Twin Elms Two. . . ."

"That was his doing?" Garrison asked.

"We have proof, back in the other building," Michael said grimly. "If you want to see it."

"And *I* might as well spend whatever time remains figuring out all I can about this Strain 8—so at least you can radio your superiors about it, warn them," Dr. Gilmore growled.

This was getting them nowhere.

"Please," Michael said reasonably. "Give us time. If all of us live through this, Dr. Gilmore and Keely will go back with you quietly. And if we don't—well, it won't matter much to you anymore, will it?"

Keely looked at him, surprised. So did her mom. He tried to ignore them; he would have to deal with their protests and arguments later.

The colonel nodded slowly. "You've got till 1 p.m. tomorrow. If you find a cure or whatever, you come with us. But you better tell the people here to get ready to evacuate quietly to the cities, or whatever happens, my CO is going to order this place blown sky-high."

"Dr. Slattery is dead," Michael protested, trying to keep the desperation out of his voice. No way would the people here leave. Especially not now. "So is his brother, Frank Slattery, the strategy guy. This place is no longer a threat to you. You don't have to destroy it."

"Novo Mundum is not part of the deal. Take it or leave it."

Michael sighed, looking down the muzzle of a very sleek, very shiny gun barrel.

"We'll take it," Liza decided for everyone.

THIRTY-SIX

ACCORDING TO DR. MACTAVISH, KEELY SHOULD HAVE BEEN IN bed. Hours ago. In fact, she made Amber *watch* Keely get undressed and get into bed. "Nothing helps the body fight infections more than a good night's sleep," the doctor had said. "It ain't just for beauty."

But Amber fell asleep long before Keely did and began to snore to boot. *That's new.*

It was hard to sleep knowing she might only have a week to live—and suffer at the end of it. *Might as well do something useful,* like her mom had said. So she slipped out and went to Dr. Slattery's lab. Keely was pretty sure her mom was also up, interviewing the dying researcher. None of the other technicians knew anything helpful; Slattery had done the main work, and when he needed anything done, he just gave exact instructions without telling anyone the details. Different amounts and proportions of something were injected into people; Chong and another technician would observe the results and report back to Slattery—who would then give out new orders. They all knew they were creating vaccines, and some had been let in a little on the October Project, but the only two people who knew exactly what was going on were dead or missing.

The lab was strange and empty, kind of like coming back to what was once a dangerous level of a video game after you cleared it. She sort of expected one of the others to be there, but Irene was probably with Diego right now. Who knew if they would even find anything useful—she might as well spend her last days with someone she loved.

Someone had done an excellent job of cleaning up the blood; Keely hadn't realized until she was farther into the room that she'd expected the floor to be sticky. She shivered at the thought—it was so casual. She lit the small candle she had taken with her and set it in the middle of Slattery's desk, far enough from his computer to be safe.

What was she thinking, really? That she could find something someone else had missed? At night? By herself? What did she expect to find—a little bottle with a label that said CURE FOR STRAIN 8? A treasure map to it? A folder labeled DR. SLATTERY'S TOP SECRET PLANS, LAID OUT IN REMARKABLE DETAIL?

Footsteps in the lab. Keely didn't react; they were Michael's. Another thing she sort of automatically knew these days. Maybe it was from spending weeks in the wilderness with him, learning instinctively what signs meant friend or outsider.

"Keely?" he called out softly.

"You couldn't sleep either, huh?" she asked, rubbing her eyes. They were beginning to ache from lack of sleep—or was that something else?

"No, I guess I had the same idea you did." He came into the candlelight, whose flame and shadows somehow managed to make him appear both older and less tired than he was. Actually, he looked pretty gorgeous. In a Johnny Depp sort of way. *How did he remember to shave during this time of crisis?* Keely found herself wondering, admiring the angles of his cheekbones.

"It's pretty useless, though, isn't it?" He sighed, leaning against the desk. "What a stupid way to end up. I've spent the last few months running from *everything*—the government, Dr. Slattery, the Slash, civilization, the government again . . . only to walk right into the deadliest mess of all."

Keely shrugged. "Shit happens when you decide to try and save the world."

Michael laughed and rubbed his head. She wished he was more like this more often. It was like the first symptom of the disease was the destruction of all the complex shields that each person hid behind. With Liza it was the little-girlishness, with Michael it was the type-A hero. Underneath it he was just a smart, nice guy who wanted to help and save everyone.

Too bad she hadn't realized it earlier. They might have gotten along better. They might have . . .

Keely was pretty sure she moved first, although in a moment it didn't matter. His hands cupped the back of her neck and he was kissing her. She pulled him closer until their legs were slightly intertwined, their bodies twisted together, awash in the flickering light of the candle.

She heard the quiet catch of his breath as the kiss deepened, and she closed her eyes and let herself go, abandoning her usual reserve, proceeding without caution. Perhaps that was the complex shield she hid behind—the cautious, smart girl who always looked before she leaped.

But not at this moment. Right now everything was about kissing Michael, feeling the comfort of being held in his arms, the sweetness of knowing he cared. With each tremor of his touch she felt a new wave of hope, hope for the world, for herself, hope that maybe these feelings that burned through her when he was near were even related to love.

She hadn't felt *this* with anyone since Eric—not even Gabe. With Gabe it had been nice, and new, and he'd been a great guy—but Michael was different. The two of them had been together since first getting to Novo Mundum, and each had seen the other at their best and worst. There was a closeness there beyond normal friendship. And it was no secret that the two of them had their own friendship apart from the rest of the group, a distinct connection.

When they broke off, Keely found herself torn between laughing and crying.

"I've wanted to do that for so long," Michael whispered.

"With me it was the train," Keely said, wiping her eyes.

"Wait—what?"

"You were pretty hot that night."

"Only *that* night?"

"Well, you're kind of an ass normally."

"Oh, thanks a lot." Michael pushed her away so that he could sink his head into her chest like a grieving child. "An ass! So what are you doing with an ass like me?"

She laughed, tipping his head up so that she could meet his eyes. "Oh, I have a few things in mind."

He rolled his eyes, then pressed his face into her again, kissing the narrow tract between her breasts.

Keely sighed. She hadn't felt this warm, safe, and *happy* since before 7—and didn't want to feel guilty about it. She sank her fingers into his hair and began to massage his scalp, shivering in response to his lips, his hands. . . .

And then she saw the glint of something behind Michael's head, next to the computer. Something glass caught by candlelight.

"Get up," she ordered, climbing off him.

"*Now* what?" Michael asked, smiling a little. "You're so full of commands, little miss. . . ."

She moved the candle closer to the computer and found several sealed beakers in what looked like a mini-terrarium, also sealed. She pulled it carefully across the desk—obviously everything was sealed for a reason. Closer inspection found writing—with a wax pencil, probably—that said *Rota (B)*.

"What the hell are those? Strain 8?" Michael asked, backing off a little. If she weren't trying to work something out in her head, Keely would have found it funny—wasn't he already exposed? What did it matter?

"Rotavirus B," she said slowly, jogging her memory. What had her mom said? A long time ago, when Bree was sick as an infant? Something about how so many different things are misdiagnosed as stomach flu when really it's something else, like food poisoning. Babies often got the real deal. Her mom's old student had helped come up with a vaccine. Rotashield or something like that. "It's a stomach bug," she explained aloud to Michael. It didn't make any sense. Why would Dr. Slattery bother with such a basically harmless virus . . . ?

Michael's eyes widened with hope—it certainly sounded like what all of them had. "'Ready to repeat with actual,'" he murmured.

"What?" Now Keely had no idea what he was talking about.

"What if Dr. Slattery tested out the whole 'salt the earth' thing with something else first—something harmless but traceable, to see how it behaved? Like your mom said the army did in the subway tunnels. To see if it could survive and stay in the dirt and water or whatever so that people coming in could get it?"

Keely nodded slowly. "Sometimes this virus contaminates whole water supplies—it can live quite happily in streams and swamps."

"Let's go get your mom," Michael suggested.

Keely nodded, then paused. "But we can get back to this later, right?"

THIRTY–SEVEN

BLEARY-EYED, EVERYONE REASSEMBLED IN LIZA'S OFFICE. SHE sat at her desk, trying to rub the sleep out of her eyes— until someone on the support staff brought her a steaming cup of real coffee. She ordered four more for the rest of them.

Every other thought was of her dad.

The moment the gun went off, the moment he fell to the floor: these images replayed in her head tirelessly on a loop. When they faded, Liza was left with a black hollow somewhere behind her mouth that extended up into her head and down into her belly. *Father killer. Patricide. I killed Dad.*

When she wasn't thinking about her dad, it was Uncle Frank. She had told the guards to capture him alive—while delaying as long as possible. They were the most shaken up of any group at Novo Mundum, the most betrayed.

But no one had seen any sign of him, not even tracks in the woods. It was like he had vanished.

Liza whispered a little prayer, knowing he had done the same thing for her every moment she was gone.

She shook her head, trying to push aside the thoughts for a few moments. Other work needed be done; she had the rest of her life to feel remorse and guilt.

Keely looked excited, a nervous expectation that combined with exhaustion made her practically vibrate. Colonel Garrison, as usual, didn't look at all put out about attending a meeting at four o'clock in the morning. He stood stock-straight and didn't move a muscle or crack a joke.

Michael passed the time waiting for Keely's mom by going over Frank's logs again. They were beginning to make more sense if what he thought was true—the key term was *ready to Repeat w/actual,* as if the first one was just a test.

Dr. Gilmore hadn't been asleep either. When the snow sprite—or whatever her name was; Keely kept calling her that—brought her and the soldier guarding her back, she looked beyond exhausted: she was shaking a little. Michael pulled a chair out for her and the guard even helped her down.

"What's wrong, Mom? Are you feeling okay?" Keely asked, looking alarmed. It didn't look like the stomach flu.

Her mom shook her head, shivering a little. "I was just

interviewing the old head of research. Through a glass wall," she added quickly. "He said they needed to speed things up after the incident with some army guys. . . ."

"What?" Garrison demanded. "What army guys?"

"I'll tell you later," Michael promised. It might not be the *truth*, but he would tell him something.

"He . . . exposed himself to the October Project. On purpose." She looked up at them all, as if wishing for the instantaneous magic of a trouble shared becoming a trouble halved. But Liza was pretty sure the sudden urge to vomit wasn't just from whatever sickness he was suffering. "I think he felt guilty. . . ."

"What a screwed-up way to commit suicide," Michael said, trying to sound grown-up and manly—but Liza could see the horror in his eyes.

"That's one of the worst things I've ever heard—" she agreed.

"Jesus Christ," Garrison swore. "What the hell kind of cult *is* this?"

"—but you said you had news about Strain 8," she added, glaring at the military man. That was one advantage she had growing up as a sort of princess, Michael thought, trying not to smile. She had "regal bearing" down pat and wasn't used to anyone interrupting or disobeying her. She just *assumed* command. And perception was everything.

"Not exactly about that, but we think we were infected by something else—rotavirus B, a version of the stomach flu." Keely held up the bottle.

"Let me see that," her mom said, taking it—but

obviously there wasn't a lot to look at, just slightly murky liquid.

"My men are vomiting their guts out because of a stomach flu?" the colonel demanded. "The kind that babies get?"

Dr. Gilmore shook her head. "This kind—B—is usually only found in China, and it affects adults; the one we have here, A, only infects babies and young children."

Michael handed Liza the part of Frank's log that talked about the missions and testing.

11/22

~~Valdes~~ *Hakata, Jabbers, Sosa, Ronson under Robeire, 12–3 o'clock Mitchell, Abrams, Flood, and Noonan under Tabori, 4–7 o'clock Diettrich Hammel Rosenberg Jonah under Chan. Water Robeire, 3, Tabori 1, Chan, 4*

Reread re: Tular

11/29

Affirmative on effects w/detainees
ready to Repeat w/actual

"See?" he said. "'Ready to repeat with actual'—like the first one is just a test."

Liza nodded. "What's a tular?" she asked, pointing at the word.

"I thought that was someone's name," Michael said, shrugging.

"No one here."

"Let me see that," Dr. Gilmore said, going over and

reading over her shoulder. "Could he be referring to tularemia? That rabbit fever disease?"

"What's so special about it?" Keely asked.

"It's considered a biological weapon," Garrison answered. "It stays in the environment a long time."

"How the hell do you know that?" Michael asked for everyone.

"I'm Special Forces," he answered with a tiny tug of his lips that might have almost been a smile. "I was one before MacCauley stepped in. Let's just say we get educated a *lot* about the things we might face in the Mideast."

Michael felt his heart sink a little. He had thought there was a chance of reasoning with the guy—standing there in his uniform, looking a little smug, he could have been an older version of Gabe. Nice boy with a career in the military, fun to party with. But James Garrison was part of the most elite and covert part of the army, probably even an assassin. Used to following horrible orders to the letter—and not failing.

"Well, it all adds up," he said aloud, trying not to be intimidated by him. *Think of Gabe.* "But some proof would be nice. We should interview all the people who went on this mission—it looks like they were also assigned to the 'real' one. Maybe they have some idea— I'll bet Tabori does."

"Make it so," Liza said, waving her hand only half ironically. She rang the bell on her desk and the snow sprite reappeared. "Gather these people and bring them to me; I need to talk to them," she said, handing her the paper. The girl nodded and ran off.

"I need to get me one of those," Dr. Gilmore said, sighing a little.

"Once you talk to them, if it turns out it's just the stomach flu or whatever," Garrison said, walking forward a little, his hand casually on his gun, "we evacuate this place and blow it sky-high—with or without anyone in it."

Liza frowned. "I remember our deal, Colonel. I'll call a meeting the moment we all find out we're going to live. Until then you can stop going on about blowing things sky-high."

"You don't understand," Michael said, desperately trying. "The people here really are trying to keep the arts and sciences alive. While everyone out there is living in fear of you, pantomiming normal life, eating rations, and terrified of accidentally breaking a law, here they teach music and write books and—"

"And breed deadly viruses, apparently."

"You can't hold people responsible for what their leader did—no one knew about his ultimate plans except his brother! *We* still don't."

Garrison shrugged and stood back into a very obvious at ease.

There must be something. Even inside the ranger. Michael knew it. Everyone had *some* chink. . . .

THIRTY-EIGHT

"OH MY GOD, WE CAN FINALLY SLEEP!" KEELY SAID THANKFULLY as she, her mom, and Michael left the room.

"And bonus: we're going to live out the rest of our days as well," her mother replied dryly.

"Maybe you missed the look of euphoria on my face," Keely said, pointing. She felt giddy and silly—being told simply that she was going to live was like receiving fantastic presents, a boyfriend, and days at the beach all at once. "I thought the whole not-going-to-die thing was pretty obvious."

Her mom shivered and Michael nodded seriously, each going through their own stages of overwhelming relief.

"Hey, I should show you around Novo Mundum,"

Keely added. In some ways, this was as close to her mom visiting her at college as she would ever get. It would be kind of exciting, showing a parent where she had lived *without* her family.

"Tomorrow," Dr. Gilmore said. "Right now I need sleep."

"Better not wait too long," Michael muttered morosely. "It's going to be gone in a few days."

"The getting-to-*live*-happily-ever-after part?" Keely pointed out, poking him on the shoulder. "Like my mom said? Are we already forgetting?"

"No, it's an incredible relief," he said, releasing a huge breath that he might have been holding somewhere within him since yesterday. His and Keely's eyes met for a moment, but she couldn't read what was there. Some strong emotion—was he feeling guilty about last night? Did he have some idea about their future? "I almost can't believe it. Something about dying from Strain 8 seemed somehow inevitable. Now—it's like I don't even know what to do."

Keely turned away, trying to act casual. "You could come to Los Angeles," she suggested. "Mom could get you travel orders."

"I can help get you situated," her mom said before pausing to think. "Assuming I haven't used up all my favors . . ."

"Yeah—hey." Keely saw Michael's eyes slip to Garrison, who was just leaving. "I think I'm just going to go back and talk to Liza, if you guys don't mind. She needs a lot of support right now."

"Sure," Keely said quickly, hoping to cover up a look

of disappointment. She had hoped Michael would jump on the possibility of heading west with her, of just being with her, but she had to remind herself he had more pressing matters on his mind.

When did I turn into such a girly freak?

"I'll see you later. Good night, Dr. Gilmore." Hands in his pockets, he turned around and left. Keely was watching him, trying to figure out what was going through his mind, when she felt her mother's hand on her arm.

"Get me to a bed. Now."

"We should probably tell Irene and Diego the good news before going to sleep," Keely said.

"Have fun with that. *I'm* going to bed." Her mom studied her in that inquisitive "mom" way, as if trying to figure out what was different about her daughter. What had changed, what had been dropped out of and added to her emotional inventory. Finally she leaned over and kissed Keely on the cheek, just as she had when she was a little girl. "Good night, Keely."

"G'night, Mom," Keely said. It was the first time in three years they had performed this ritual. It felt a little rusty, but—*right.*

THIRTY-NINE

MICHAEL KNOCKED ON THE DOOR AS HE WALKED IN, THE OTHER hand still shoved deeply into his pocket. Part of him felt like he was seeing the principal.

"What?" Liza looked up, annoyed, then saw who it was. "Oh, hey," she relented. "I thought you were going to bed."

"Just wanted to see how you were doing . . ." How could he say it? How could he ask her how she was dealing with shooting her own father?

"I have a *lot* 'to do,'" she said, pointing at a pile of papers on her desk. It looked like a list of everyone at Novo Mundum, alphabetically by work group. "Somehow between now and whenever Garrison finally loses his temper, I've got to come up with a way to get everyone to leave as quietly, meekly, and in as organized a fashion as possible."

"Why didn't you fight more?" Michael asked, curious, slipping into the chair opposite her.

"I only saw four soldiers with the colonel," Liza pointed out. "That doesn't mean there aren't a dozen more waiting out in the woods. Even if we chose to stay and fight, all they have to do is call for reinforcements." She frowned, saying aloud what she had obviously been thinking for some time. "My dad was loyal to the *concept* of Novo Mundum. I care more about its people—and any engagement with Garrison would result in a bloodbath. I'll continue to try and reason with him, of course, but we should have a backup plan for getting everyone out."

It might not be the choice he would have made, but Michael couldn't help admiring her. She really did care about the people who had sworn their loyalty to her and would do anything she could to protect them—even if they didn't like it.

"Liza," he said, trying to think of the right words, "you're doing the right thing. You *did* the right thing."

"Michael, I killed my dad." She put her hand to her forehead as if to wipe away something, but there were no tears—just a haunted darkening of her eyes.

I should never have taken her away from Novo Mundum. Even as he thought it, Michael knew it was a ridiculous notion. They had to leave, she chose to go, thousands, maybe millions of lives might be depending on them—all of which had been saved with the death of Dr. Slattery.

It just shouldn't have been Liza who'd shot him.

"I know," he whispered. "I am so sorry."

"Thanks," she said with a glum smile. "But not as sorry as I am."

FORTY

THE NEXT MORNING WAS BRIGHT AND SUNNY, AS IF THE WEATHER had cleared with the events of the night before. The whole day felt like good news; when Irene and Diego walked hand in hand to the dining hall, it felt like they were at the dawn of a beautiful, clean new world. The snow sparkled like sugar crystals and Mundians were actually *playing* in it—some adults as well as the kids. The time of mourning was over for them—or at least on hold. Liza had declared it a day off for everyone, partially to begin secretly planning the evacuation of Novo Mundum.

They don't know the truth yet, Irene thought sadly. She hoped that they could enjoy their last days at Novo Mundum without too much worry, that the rangers would keep a tight lid on the plan until Liza's meeting.

"What do you want to do now?" Irene asked, giving Diego a playful kiss on the cheek.

"Eat breakfast. Then maybe throw you into the snow." He paused, thinking. "Maybe throw you into the snow *first.*"

Irene laughed. It was so nice to see him back to normal. "I mean *after . . .* all this."

Diego shrugged. "Try to escape the soldiers, maybe? Find someplace safe on the fringes of the Big Empty—a nice village or town or something?"

Irene tried to hide her look of disappointment.

"I know you wanted to go to L.A.," he said gently, cupping her chin in his hand. "But first of all, you weren't invited. These soldier boys are going to put you wherever they put everyone else. Second, I'm trying to compromise here. I'll live in your crap-ass civilization with its mad scientists, soldiers, and deadly viruses—if you let me have a little bit of isolation. I am *not* going back to one of those cities."

Irene nodded. She knew he was right—real relationships, real long-term ones, were all *about* compromise. It was just that she hoped he would magically change his mind. Dr. Gilmore was so nice to her and Irene was *sure* she could use her influence to get her to L.A., maybe take her on as an apprentice or something. And, she realized, she didn't want to leave Michael and Keely and Amber or even Jonah forever. In this world of broken communications, it wasn't like they could just pick up a phone.

The day seemed a little gaudy now. She swallowed

back her disappointment and squeezed his hand. He kissed her, but it wasn't all better. They continued on to the dining hall silently.

Why does this suddenly seem a thousand times harder than when we were fighting for our lives in the woods?

FORTY-ONE

KEELY SAW IRENE AND DIEGO COME INTO THE DINING HALL and cheerily waved them over. Just like old times—almost.

"Looks like something's wrong in Mr. and Mrs. Perfectsville," Amber muttered, licking her fingers for the little bit of fat on the sort-of muffins that were being offered that morning. Apparently Keely's old roomie had been up and about a whole lot more since they'd all gotten back—to Dr. MacTavish's dismay. But they all took it slowly with her, using a wheelchair whenever possible, and so far she was fine.

Amber and her mom had gotten along surprisingly well, Keely was glad to see. Dr. Gilmore used to have some surprisingly questionable things to say about kids from South Central, and Keely had worried a lot about introducing her young pregnant-teen best friend. But they were both on good behavior so far.

It would have been a genuinely good morning if the person rounding out their party wasn't Colonel Garrison.

"You were invited here too?" he asked, tearing off a piece of his protein bar—though he politely shunned the other "commune food," he graciously accepted a mug of weak tea.

"Not exactly," Amber said. "Long story."

Irene and Diego finally made it over to the table and slid in next to the others. "So," Diego began with a smile-ish flash of teeth to the colonel. "Find any secret rooms yet? Hidden agendas? Brain-altering drugs or ideals?"

"You're a very angry man," Garrison answered, smiling back over his mug. "But since you asked, no. This place is surprisingly . . . pleasant," he said with a growl-catch in his throat, as if it hurt him to admit it.

"I showed him the classrooms this morning," Keely said, hoping the two guys would simmer down. She gave a quick sideways look to Irene. "And around the dorms."

"I thought it was a cult too, you know," her mom said, staring into the distance and picturing who knew what. "I guess it sort of is, by the psychological definition. But with Slattery gone, it really could be a good *commun*ity."

Garrison shrugged. "Still trying to convince me?"

"You know, we were going to try to talk to you back in Houston," Keely said slowly.

"Really?" Garrison seemed genuinely surprised.

"Yeah, it's kind of ironic," Keely said with a wan smile. "When we found out that *something* was going on with Strain 8 and Dr. Slattery, we were going to tell you about it—everyone had good things to say about you. About you letting the shops stay open on the south side instead of forcing them to relocate, about how you were a little more . . . understanding than the other district supervisors."

She saw his jaw and brow set—whether from anger or something else, Keely couldn't tell. There was some strong emotion going on behind his cold face, however.

"What stopped you?" he asked.

"Red Haven," Diego answered for her. *Oh, crap, please let him shut up. . . .* Irene seemed to be kicking him under the table. Amber and her mom exchanged confused looks. "It was a community like this one—without the mad scientist—in Colorado. When the army ordered them out, they refused, and they blew the place 'sky-high.'"

"We thought it was Novo Mundum at first," Keely murmured, looking up at Amber. Her roommate's eyes widened as she realized what that must have meant to them.

"I had nothing to do with that," Garrison said, again neither confirming it as a good act nor denying it as horrible.

"You're part of the system, my friend," Dr. Gilmore said before Diego could.

"Okay, as long as we're going to 'do this,' let me

make something clear," the colonel said, setting his mug down with a quiet but solid *whump.* "I *am* more lenient than the other district supervisors. *Any* other. My background in the government lets me work the system better than other flunkies and grunts, and as a result, the people in Houston have slightly greater freedom than the rest of the country. You think I *like* what I do? You think I *like* what's going on out there? This isn't the America I signed on to serve.

"And every minute I'm *here,* on this stupid-ass mission, the *government* guy they assigned as my replacement is undoing every bit of good I tried to do."

He glared at all of them, and Keely could see that this was the real James Garrison coming out, the one behind both the easy demeanor and the soldier mask he had been wearing since he arrived. "So while you all are concerned about the thousand or so people here, *I've* got the fate of several *hundred* thousand depending on me. And the sooner I wrap this up, the sooner I can get back to making sure that no one gets executed for stealing food."

And with that he stood up, gave a polite nod, and stormed off.

"Right guy," Keely said sadly. "Wrong time and place."

FORTY-TWO

LIZA LOOKED UP TO SEE SOMEONE FROM HER STAFF—DIRK?—hovering anxiously in front of her. "Yes?" she asked, a little crossly. She looked at the clock—8 a.m. already. They had five hours to look for the people on her list. Novo Mundum wasn't that big. "Where are they?"

"That's just it, Liza," the boy said nervously. "We couldn't find any of them. They're gone."

FORTY-THREE

"WHAT DO YOU MEAN, THEY'RE GONE?" GARRISON DEMANDED.

They were all back in Liza's office: Michael, Keely, her mom, Irene, Diego, Garrison, and two of his men. It looked like the new leader of Novo Mundum was going to have her face permanently etched into annoyance. Quite a change from the wide-eyed girl who'd snuck into Michael's room in a silk bathrobe. In some ways, this one was a lot more likable.

"All of them. Gone." Liza showed him the list. "According to Henning, they went out on the last mission Frank ordered. Which was probably to disperse the *real* virus into the ground. *Because,*" she said wearily, sinking into her chair, "I told them to continue with all routine standing orders."

"This isn't routine," Keely pointed out.

"I'll bet it was Tabori," Michael muttered, taking the sheet and looking at it. "I'll bet she had some idea of what was going on—and was determined to carry out her beloved commander's plan."

"We have to find them—and stop them," Garrison said, swearing.

"Why?" Liza asked. "We traveled all this way to stop my dad from launching a viral bomb against the world. Turns out his main plan was just to saturate the area around Novo Mundum. So we get vaccinated—what's the big deal?"

"Streams flow downhill," Diego said quietly. "And although I don't understand everything you all have said about it, can't Strain 8 survive for a *long* time in the environment?"

"And what if someone walks through—and lives long enough to bring it back with him?" Dr. Gilmore pointed out. "If the incubation period is half a week, he could infect an entire town . . . which could go on to infect the entire area . . ."

". . . like *The Stand,*" Michael finished. *"Again."*

"Okay, I'll take my men and go," Garrison said, pulling out his walkie-talkie. "But there are only five of us. I could really use some help."

"I'll order all our scouts to assemble immediately." Liza nodded, ringing her bell. "If we're not too late . . ."

"I'll go," Diego volunteered. "You need someone good in the woods like me."

Everyone looked expectantly at Michael.

"What? Are you insane? Remember the *last* time I was in the wilderness?" He said it jokingly and was glad to see even Diego crack a smile. It was the first time he had ever admitted a weakness about anything to anyone—in front of a *group* of people. He really would get in the way. "I'll stay here and help Liza coordinate things."

"All right, then, let's go." Liza arose, looking every inch the woman in power she needed to be.

FORTY-FOUR

THE WOOD WAS WHITE AND BROWN WITH SNOW AND THE DARK bark of trees; the green of pines was only visible if you looked up. And Diego didn't.

It was silent and smelled good and he was *hunting,* something he excelled at, something he could lose himself in. This was the most important thing he had ever stalked—so funny that the fate of what remained of the rest of the human race relied on a tracker in the woods. Not decisions in the cities or shoot-outs in the streets.

He had picked up the trail about ten minutes after being sent out, and though he didn't need to check his compass for direction—he could do that without the help from tools, thank you—he used it to make sure he had the right guy and wasn't following someone else's mark.

There was the snapping of a branch somewhere up ahead, the sort of step-on and slip-off noise someone inexperienced in the woods would make trying to navigate obstacles covered in snow that took on unfamiliar shapes. He was maybe twenty feet away, at the top of a short, steep hill that looked like it was the back side of a gorge. *He's going to drop the vial into the riverbed,* Diego realized.

He began to walk more stealthily; these jumpy guards were more likely to shoot first and ask questions later. Who knew what Tabori had told them? Diego kept behind tree trunks and stayed in the zebra shadows the white morning sun made through the trees. The only noise he made was a near-silent crunch as he stepped through the snow. Ten more feet. Five . . .

And then he caught sight of who it was.

And broke a twig in his astonishment.

The guard turned around—

It was Jonah.

FORTY-FIVE

"YOU WILL BE GOING AFTER TURK MITCHELL," MICHAEL SAID, handing the woman in her mid-thirties a compass and a rough map. "Your last scouting mission was northeast toward Hilldale, so we're sending you to 2:30 on the map. Did Dr. Gilmore debrief you on safe handling of the virus?"

The woman gave a curt nod—unlike many they were sending out, Pela had been a guide at national parks for serious backcountry hikers. Most of the others were ex-military—but she had just as good a chance of finding someone in the woods as they did, maybe better.

They had already sent out about thirty people in all directions of the compass; he'd taken the northeast quadrant, Keely three to six, Liza six to nine, and Regina, one of the Novo Mundum guards, had taken the north-west. If anyone was watching via satellite, he would see a slow spreading warmth—like a rash—as they sent wave after wave of people out from NM. *Hopefully someone's looking away from his desk,* Michael thought as Regina left.

"Ow!" He jumped as something sharp was jabbed into his upper arm.

"Stay still," Dr. MacTavish ordered, emptying the rest of a syringe into him. "I'm giving you a dose of the vaccine."

"You could give me a *warning* while you're at it," he growled, indicating to the next volunteer the compass and the paper he should take.

FORTY-SIX

"JONAH," DIEGO SAID, SINCE IT WAS OBVIOUS HIS COVER WAS blown. Both were too stunned to grasp the situation immediately. "What are you doing here? You were supposed to be someone named Diettrich."

"We switched," Jonah said, recovering first. "I'm not so good in the woods; he gave me the easier assignment. What are you doing here?"

"We came back." Diego thought quickly. How could he explain the truth—fast—in such a way that Jonah would actually *listen?* He had no reason to; the last time they'd met, Diego had been shooting at him. "You know you're about to dump Strain 8 into the water?"

Jonah looked down into the palm of his hand

wonderingly. He was already holding the vial, Diego was horrified to see. Ready to toss it.

"I . . . had some idea," he said slowly.

"You know that if you dump it into the water, everything downstream gets it too, right?"

"So?" Jonah said, again slowly and distracted. "We'll be safe."

"You'll be killing *millions* if it gets back to civilization!" Diego yelled. "Jonah, can we put our differences aside for a moment? I know you don't want to do that."

"It was Dr. Slattery's plan," Jonah said stubbornly.

What was the lie they had all agreed on? That Frank had killed his brother? Why, exactly? Had they decided that it was all Frank's idea? "A lot of this was his crazy brother's thing—Frank's, *not* Dr. Slattery's."

Jonah just stared at him. He wasn't stupid—he might be ignorant of the real cause of Paul's death, but he wasn't buying the rest of it. "You going to shoot at me? Again?"

"If they had taken us back, I would have been used as a guinea pig—of course I wasn't going to let them do that!"

"You were going to die anyway," he said uncertainly.

"Do I *look* dead?" Diego demanded. "Are you listening to yourself? Have they really turned you into a mass murderer?"

"If people left us alone, they'd be fine," Jonah mumbled. Then he straightened up and looked Diego in the eye. "You *left,* anyway—you don't get a say in the future of Novo Mundum. You had your chance—they didn't even call you—and you *blew* it! You were willing to *kill* me to get away!"

"Jonah, Novo Mundum probably would have *executed* Michael and Keely—and yes, Irene!"

Jonah's eyes burned at this. He slowly held out his arm, the vial still in his palm. "You should have stayed in the woods, where you belong."

"Well, there's one thing we both agree on," Diego muttered. Then he leapt at Jonah.

It was an old-fashioned football tackle—but he pushed his shoulder as hard as he could into Jonah's belly and grabbed his arm to keep the test tube from flying. Jonah was bigger than he was, though, and with a good kick to Diego's side he rolled out of the way, curling the arm with the vial as he went.

Diego threw himself back on top of him, trying to smash his forehead into Jonah's nose. But the other boy spasmed and the two foreheads crushed into each other instead, stunning both of them.

As soon as his vision cleared, Diego forced his knee up onto Jonah's arm, crushing his elbow into the dirt, trying to get him to drop the vial. They struggled perilously close to the edge of the ravine now—just a few more inches and Jonah would be able to drop the glass vial onto the rocks below.

Jonah grabbed a handful of dirt with his other hand and threw it into Diego's face.

It took all of his effort not to react by letting go, but he was distracted enough for Jonah to throw all of his weight to the side, pushing Diego off him. He rolled away, tucking the hand that held the test tube so it wouldn't get smashed.

Diego wheezed, pretending he was out of breath. "Think—about—what—you're—*doing!*"

At the last moment he forced himself to twist, an old wrestling move, and spun around on his hips so he faced Jonah. With all of his effort, he kicked out.

The fleshy *thunk* was horrible—it sounded like he had broken a rib—but not as horrible as what came next.

Jonah stumbled backward, off balance, looking surprised for a moment—

Then pitched into the gorge below.

FORTY–SEVEN

THE MOOD BACK AT NOVO MUNDUM WAS MIXED.

Irene burst into tears on hearing the news. But she didn't move away when Diego held her.

Keely—and everyone else—was more worried about the effect of losing the vial. After looking at maps and many long discussions with her mom, the group came to the conclusion that it wasn't the *worst* of the ones to have lost—most of the stream wound up in a lake not far from NM, but not in the river itself. Still, it was south of them. . . .

"Here," Liza said formally, handing a box to Colonel Garrison.

"What's this?" he asked in surprise.

"It's forty doses of the vaccine for Strain 8 and one live sample. I know it's not a lot, but Dr. Gilmore tells me that you can use it to make more," she answered, with a resigned smile. "You should probably give it to everyone within a hundred miles of Twin Elms Two— and anyone downstream of us."

Garrison's eyes widened in surprise. "You could have destroyed this and I never would have known."

"Novo Mundum is about saving the future of humanity," Liza said with dignity. "*Not* about killing millions of people."

Keely couldn't help glowing with pride a little—Liza was really growing into her role, into a *person*. Wise and kind—everything her father wasn't.

"It's a hard bargain you drive," the colonel finally said slowly, coming to some sort of conclusion he had been wrestling with.

"What?" Liza asked, surprised.

"But I guess I have no choice but to give in. Millions of lives might depend on it."

"What are you talking about?"

Keely and Michael looked at each other, suddenly getting it at the same time.

"You understand that we had to," Michael said, playing along quickly. "We can't let you discover the secret location of our community."

"We'll get the vaccine once I and my men are back in Texas?" Garrison said with a straight face.

"I *just* gave it to y— Oh," Liza said, finally understanding as the three of them glared at her. "Oh, uh, yeah. The moment you're over the border, we'll have someone deliver it to you."

"What can I do? My hands are tied," Garrison said with a toothy smile.

"What made you change your mind?" Keely asked curiously.

"You," he answered, shrugging. "Seeing this place. Knowing that it's out there, somewhere, this little piece of whatever it is, free from MacCauley—well, it'll make the days go easier. And like I said, I have better work to do than to spend time relocating y'all."

Working within the system—to beat the system, Keely noted, shaking her head. It was kind of crazy—if they *had* told Garrison in the beginning, it probably all would have ended badly. So many little decisions and small discoveries could tip the balance and change the future—scary, really.

"At least you found what you came for," her mom said, coming forward with her hands up as if her wrists were bound.

"Yeah, you two are coming too." He indicated Keely and Michael. "That part of the deal stays."

"Wait—me? Why me?" Michael demanded.

"Because you along with mom and daughter here are obviously troublemakers. I don't really see the rest of them—no offense—getting together to do everything you've done without your leadership and influence," Garrison said with a tight, unfunny grin. "I think you could get into a lot of trouble out here in the Big Empty—I think I'd like you where someone could keep an eye on you."

Keely grinned at Michael, and he sort of smiled

back. It was kind of nice to be thought of as dangerous by a Special Forces Ranger.

"Well, I gotta stay anyway until this guy pops," Amber said, trying to sound cheerful. "Oh, crap," she suddenly added. "Does that mean it's time for goodbyes?"

FORTY-EIGHT

IRENE AND DIEGO SAT ON THE EDGE OF THE STAGE IN A DARK-
ened lecture hall, having a winter's picnic of bread and
cheese and sliced turnip while the wind whistled outside. Even Irene didn't particularly feel like joining
everyone else in the loud, crowded dining hall for
lunch, though usually Diego was the antisocial one.

Her stomach was as frozen as the sidewalks outside,
thoughts whistling through her head like the wind
around the rafters. *What. Next.*

"Hey," Diego began slowly, trying to be casual while
crunching through some probably indigestible crust. *I
don't want to fight about L.A. Not again,* Irene thought
sadly. "What if we . . . stayed here?"

She dropped her sandwich in surprise.

"I mean, I have mixed feelings about this place," he said with a faint smile. "But it's definitely isolated—and not like a city at all. I can go into the woods anytime I want. Hell, I could definitely teach some of these educated gomers a thing or two about hunting and scouting." His face softened. "And you could learn under Dr. MacTavish and help Amber with her baby . . . and you'd be with your dad and brother, once we found them."

Irene couldn't believe she was hearing this. She'd been so focused on the fight, on what she couldn't have, that it had never even occurred to her to stay. Or that Diego would offer it.

"I would *love* to," she said, blinking back tears.

He reached over and squeezed her hand. "But I'm not living in a dorm with some random loser," he added with a smile. "*Or* with your family. No offense."

"I'll apply for off-campus housing," Irene promised. Then she leaned over and kissed him—

And stayed there with Diego, long after lunchtime was over.

FORTY-NINE

"I haven't been on a plane in years," Michael said, looking out the window of the jet as the sound of whirring engines began to hum.

"Me neither." Keely fished an old SkyMall catalog out of the seat pocket, amazed that though there were no safety instructions, this piece of commercialism had survived. "Mom, apparently, is the big traveler now." Her mother, in the seat across the aisle, just grunted.

"I've always wanted to go to L.A. . . ." he murmured. "Ever since my mom watched *Melrose.*"

"You're going to love it," Keely promised him, eyes sparkling. "Well, except for the curfews and tanks on the street. But we can still go to the ocean, and there are palm trees. . . ."

"You're really going back to school?" he asked, as if the idea had little appeal.

She shrugged. "Even if it wasn't the law, I want to. I hate to use that 'now more than ever' crap, but even a little education will go a long way now. Just because we're not at NM doesn't mean we can't try to do what they're doing, individually. I *want* to read *Beowulf* and analyze it." Her face darkened. "And . . . I think a lot more science would be a good thing. Somebody's running around out there with a jillion other deadly diseases—we're going to have to deal with that someday."

"Yeah, I've been worried about that too," Michael said, running a hand through his hair. "I don't think things are anywhere *near* over yet, and you're right. You need to chisel out your skills. We all need to make ourselves better soldiers. But for now, I'll be just fine in the land of hot showers and *Buffy* reruns." He lowered his voice. "I can probably get a job without your mother's help. I appreciate the offer, but you should tell her not to worry about me. I've done all right for myself so far." He flashed her a confident, glittering smile.

"Oh *yeah*," Keely said, flipping through the magazine. "Giving your cozy life up for a complete nut jar who is now *queen* of the nut jars. That was a great move. Then you tried to score high with the lunatic leader of a cult *days* after you met him. And . . . do I have to reminisce over the Big Empty days? All that fun in the snow . . ."

"Don't remember much about that," he said. "That was my psychotic phase, wasn't it?"

She let her eyes open wider, enjoying the game. "Is that what you call it? Sort of like Picasso's Blue Period?"

"Sort of. Okay, maybe I could use a little help, but aren't you a harsh critic?"

"I *know* you. I've seen you at your best and worst. If you try to pull your Michael-Bishop-king-of-the-world crap around *me* . . ."

"I should expect to get taken down a few pegs. Got it. And you . . ."

She turned to him, his eyes flashing, his face just inches from hers. "Promise me you won't go back to hiding behind that aloof, smart-girl facade."

"I don't hide. . . ."

He pressed his face closer until he was in her space, his nose touching hers, with Keely unable to look away. "Don't play cute. Just be yourself, Keely. Intelligent and feeling. Keep the connection between here"—he gently touched the side of her head, then placed his hand right under her collarbone, near her heart—"and here."

Keely felt so moved at his perceptiveness, at his ability to see through all the insane events battering them, to see through everything and find her.

"I get it," she said. "You go for those smart, quiet types."

"Smart and sexy," he corrected, pressing his lips against hers in a kiss that stole her breath away. She heard herself groan as she felt his hand move along her thigh. Opening her lips to him, she reached over to cup his shoulder, smooth her hands over his chest.

She felt like she could stay in Michael's arms forever, but for now, they did have a few hours to kill on this plane ride.

"Ahem," Dr. Gilmore said, coughing. "If you two think you're going to be sleeping in the same room in *my* house, you can just forget it right now."

That froze their hands in place, ending the kiss.

Keely waited till her mother turned away, then leaned close to whisper in Michael's ear. "Don't worry. We'll just have to take it out of the house."

EPILOGUE

WITH HIS CLOTHES FINALLY DRY, IT WAS TIME TO MOVE ON.

Jonah re-shouldered the small bag he had been given by Tabori—not much in it, a little food and a knife, but it would have to do.

He set off east because the sun rose that way and walked through the woods, the glass test tube in his hand outstretched in front of him, as if it were guiding the way.